SEPTEMBER
AND THE
NIGHT

Maica Rafecas (Llorenç del Penedès, 1987) is a social educator, anthropologist and writer who has won numerous awards for her work. *September and the Night* is her first novel. She has also published the poetry collection, *Blanc breu* (Bromera, 2017). *El setembre i la nit* was chosen as one of the nine finalists for the Premi Òmnium a la Millor Novel·la de l'any (Òmnium Prize for the Best Novel of the Year).

Megan Berkobien is an educator, organizer and translator from Catalan and Spanish. She founded the Emerging Translators Collective, a collaborative micropress based on horizontal publication models for translators, at the University of Michigan, where she gained a PhD in Comparative Literature on (e)co-translation.

María Cristina Hall is a Mexican-American poet and translator working between English, Spanish and Catalan. She is a doctoral student in Political and Social Sciences at Universidad Nacional Autónoma de México (UNAM) and holds a master's degree in translation from the Universitat Pompeu Fabra. She studied creative writing at Columbia University.

This translation has been published in Great Britain
by Fum d'Estampa Press Limited 2023
001

English language translation © Megan Berkobien and María Cristina Hall, 2023

The moral rights of the author and translator have been asserted
Set in Minion Pro

Printed and bound by Great Britain by CMP UK Ltd.
A CIP catalogue record for this book is available from the British Library

ISBN: 978-1-913744-45-8

This work was translated with the help of a grant from the Institut Ramon Llull.

**institut
ramon llull**
Catalan Language and Culture

SEPTEMBER AND THE NIGHT

MAICA RAFECAS

Translated by

MEGAN BERKOBIEN &
MARÍA CRISTINA HALL

SEPTEMBER
AND THE
NIGHT

For Eudald

THE LOOKOUT POINT

He sounded the horn.

He could make out Samira's silhouette moving inside the house. She must have heard him, but she was still getting ready. Bringing a cigarette to his lips, he peered at himself in the rear-view mirror, at the blond, sweaty strands of hair and the moles on his forehead. She'd like him all the same, in that usual way of hers — as a friend, a lover, someone with whom things would always be okay. Dust had settled on the glove compartment, radio and steering wheel, but the two of them were close enough that it didn't matter. As he waited, the exhaust pipe pumped out fumes, his car noisy as a city street. With one hand, he brought the lighter up to the end of his cigarette; with the other, he beckoned.

December had now imposed itself. He saw her shuffle out the front door in a rush, as if his white Corsa were drawing her. The black leggings she wore to lounge around the house, her even darker, tousled hair — everything looked good on her. And messy hair suited him too, he thought, but there was no need to make an effort anyway, since there'd be nobody else at the lookout point by the chapel. As she moved to open the door, he raised his cigarette finger to greet her, knowing that her white smile against her brown skin would make him melt. Hello, Jan. Hi, Samira. Lucky they could go out, chat, shoot the shit; lucky the unending employment crisis would melt him away too, but differently.

They crossed Vilarer in second gear, without having to slow down much at stop signs and pedestrian crossings, not even at crossroads, since kids didn't really play outside anymore. They passed the last roundabout and picked up speed on the grey, potholed asphalt. Half a tire jut off the narrow road — an age-old goat path, now tarred over. Slaps on the knee, small talk, laughter and quiet. They stopped at the petrol station. Samira stepped out of the car and went into the store, quickly returning with a couple of cans.

As he'd waited outside her house, he'd picked up on the scent of cous-cous spices in the air. Her dark, curly hair — rounded like a treetop by night — bounced as she ran out the door. She must have really wanted to get her hands on some beer. He knew that her parents would have wanted her to turn out differently but, luckily, they weren't all that strict anymore. Thirty years had made her an adult, and Morocco was close yet far away. But what did he care, now that they were on their way to the lookout point together — if only for a little while, even if the car was covered in dust. She flashed a smile, her lips plump like a full moon.

He fixed his gaze on the condensation forming on the icy cans, like the perspiration on her back, the sweat between her breasts, the wetness between her legs... He remembered the summer. It was as if time had stood still; maybe it was the employment crisis. And Samira's skin was smooth and dark; his, pale and covered in moles. The sound of the door shutting made him lose his train of thought. Her eyes said, "Let's go," and she wrapped her hands around the dripping cans.

He drove well over the speed limit while she propped her feet up on the glove compartment, knees in the air, steadying herself as they spun past the potholes, around the turns and roundabouts. She laughed wildly and cracked open the can while the forest at the water's edge flashed past them and the pine trees ahead of the lookout point concealed the setting sun as best they could. And after laughing and speeding and passing the deep woods, riding along dirt roads in first gear, foot on the clutch, they parked at the lookout point by the hermit's chapel, the Foix River and the thicket and the orioles — the one facing the dark vineyards in that seemingly normal December — with the peak of Montmell crowning the horizon.

He couldn't bring himself to talk about the news that his father had just shared, or about how much he was dreading their family lunch the next day. Nor did he want to say that he felt like a loser because he was thirty, couldn't find a job and lived with his father at the close of that wildly uncertain 2006. He couldn't even make some clichéd comment about what the hell it was that they were doing there. Because she had worse news to share.

"I'm moving to Canada."

And she said it without meeting his gaze, staring out at the vineyards at their feet, beyond them the chapel and the swamp bearing witness, and the animals that chased and fought and killed each other on the Foix Mountains near Cal Balaguer, and the un-shingled houses and the roads lined with brush. He couldn't believe it. And she'd said it without even glancing his way. Was she sorry to leave? What did she want him to say? It was as if the dark sky were about to fall down on him. But it wouldn't. He made an effort to stop thinking about it. She hadn't said a thing, and they were sheltered there together as the zephyrs of December blew outside.

Samira's bare feet rested on the dashboard, and she rubbed the back of her head with the arm she was leaning on. She held the can in her other hand and stared out at the horizon, at Montmell, the Twin Mountains and Castellot and all the hills along the blue riverbank. There was the brown and burgundy plain between them and the mountain, beneath her bare feet, and the distant Vilarer belltower's green steeple — a colour impossible to confuse with the end-of-year vines. Jan took in the silence as if it meant goodbye.

Llobeta Vineyard — which Anaïs didn't want their father to sell to developers who would devastate the land (he could just picture how his older sister would take the news) — looked like a black dot at the base of Les Bessones, the Twin Mountains. Perhaps the barking and crickets and wild hogs could be heard down there, but not from up here. Up here at the lookout point, there wasn't a sound. He was alone with Samira, a cliff before them, a thicket behind them, a big moon and that first shy star at sunset. A quiet that had been prepared for the two of them alone.

What was she looking for in Montreal? Was she sure she wanted to leave? She said yes, that there was no work in the region and that a crisis was looming. And who would want to hire an anthropologist who'd worked as a lifeguard at the town pool? Who would hire a literature major who'd poured coffee at the local bar? Literature wouldn't turn a profit, anthropology was obscure and vice versa.

"And you're going with no savings?" he asked, thinking, don't let her leave, let her stay here.

"They offered me a fellowship," she said, drying her palms on her thighs.

"A fellowship?"

"To do research and teach anthropology," she said, still rubbing her hands on her leggings. She huddled up in her big, wool sweater and drew closer to him.

Jan nodded as he listened. And he kept thinking, don't let her leave, let her stay here. But he couldn't say it, it would be too trite and seem like he wanted something more from her, and she'd always scoffed at romantic love. Best to keep quiet, swallow his beer, wait for the right moment to press himself against her lips. Because who knew when he'd get another chance?

There was the foam in his mouth, which he was ready to swallow so he could plead with her not to go. There were the momentary hues of sunset cloaking the desiccated grape leaves on the plain below. There was Jan's hand on the tight curls at the nape of Samira's neck, and Samira's hand on the denim covering

Jan's thigh. There was suddenly only one seat in use. And the steering wheel, which wouldn't bother Samira because Jan had reclined the seat. He'd lain underneath her, wrapped in her body, the colour of wet earth, labyrinthine hair the colour of night.

There was Jan, passive, with Samira riding him, her head pressed against the car roof. The ghost of her voice saying she was moving far away. She was leaving. There was a strange pact in the biting cold. Friend. Lover. A childhood bond that would never be at risk. A one-way ticket to Montreal. She could be gone a long time, so he might as well touch her and let himself be touched. There was Jan's love, like silence. He loved her and wouldn't tell her; he loved her and she'd leave but it was all the same because, right then and there, they were alone. They fucked. There was everything that had been conjured up by that love, purposefully and without warning. A cliff, a thicket, the moon, a star and the quiet. And Samira's parents weren't strict. There were passing fads, commitment like the smallest star, convention like a fleeting eclipse. They were fucking. The day would come when they wouldn't even be able to afford condoms. They were making love. The day would come when the landscape no longer stretched out before them because some grey warehouses would stand in its place — the kind of place you run away from.

BREAKDOWNS

A sudden jolt broke through the stillness in the train cabin as Anaïs contemplated the swiftly passing landscape. The train seemed to be breaking down. And it wasn't the first jolt of that already bumpy morning, either. Her father's request for a family meal confirmed her earlier sense of impending doom. The bad news would no doubt dominate the conversation. Everyone would say their piece, then she'd have to defend her family's dignity. Who else, if not her? Her father was getting old, and Jan's head was in the clouds.

The government was planning a compulsory purchase of the land in order to build a logistics centre, bringing an end to farming in the area. And Llobeta Vineyard was among the affected farms. Hers! And her grandfather's, although it belonged to her father now. The vineyard, with its little dry-stone hut that they now used for a shed, the carob and almond trees, its crestline, the slope and mistral wind. They would buy out the various owners, but they would also wipe out all her grandfather's work — thankfully, he wasn't there to witness it — as well as her father's and everyone else's. Something that couldn't be recorded, bought, or even understood by just anyone. And amidst all those thoughts, Anaïs's mind coiled up like a tendril, her forehead resting against the trembling glass.

Anxious to get to Vilarer, she thought about how picking up her daughter from her ex's house had turned into its own kind of odyssey: getting up early on Sunday morning to catch the train, dealing with the cold and stormy trip to Gelida... She was tired, but Foix seemed even more so. And who knew what time that father of hers had put her to bed? Foix said they'd spent all Saturday playing video games, eating only croquettes and fries with ketchup and mayonnaise. And who knew what she'd kept to herself about that father of hers? On top of that, once this journey came to an end, she'd have to keep her composure at the family lunch. And put up with everyone's remarks about her decision to separate. Her little girl was seven and still didn't understand. How could she tell her daughter that she'd grown bored of marriage and was now happier than ever? What worried her more was that no one in her family seemed to understand. "Anaïs, look at you just abandoning the father of your child," her own father would say. "This is unheard of, Anaïs, and in your forties," Aunt Empar would remark. "I just don't get it, Anaïs, he treated you so well!" Jan would say. And sitting there on the train, she cursed her little brother under her breath, wondering why being treated well shouldn't just be the most normal thing in the world.

Foix wanted to fog up the windowpane and draw on it. And right before taking a deep breath, her mouth up close to the glass, she said "I'm thirsty," and pulled away from the glass to curl up into the seat. Anaïs ignored her. "I'm thirsty." More silence. "Mama, why aren't you listening to me? Papa's better than you." Anaïs rummaged around in her bag, found a notebook and pencil, and gave them to her. "Be quiet and draw."

Her eyelids grew heavy as she scanned a book of poems that Jan had lent her. And she thought it was a shame, having time to read but not being able to because the train was lulling her to sleep. Had she managed to finish it, she could have returned it that day at lunch. Her head wasn't all that clear either, what with the warehouse that they called "The Logistics Centre" — just wonderful, she thought — and her separation. It was easier to stare out at the horizon and empty her mind of thoughts.

The landscape flew by and the mountain of Montserrat grew small beyond the glass, bump after bump. Foix finished her drawing and pointed to the vineyard she'd drawn, saying it was Llobeta Vineyard. Afterwards, she pointed to the girl and said it was her. Then she pointed to the old man wearing a beret and espadrilles and said it was Great-Grandpa Pau and that she'd seen him in the vineyard and he'd told her stories from the olden days. Then Anaïs got mad at her and raised her voice. It couldn't be, he had died twenty years beforehand and she couldn't have met him. And what had gotten into her? The dead don't come back and old people don't speak because no one listens to them at that age. What had she got up to at her father's house, what could they possibly be teaching her at school that would lead her to imagine such things? What would Grandpa Magí think? And Uncle Jan? What was Foix thinking? Anaïs said that Foix had embarrassed her in front of the people on the train. And she was getting dizzy with each new bump, and feeling dizzier still because Foix wasn't behaving and loved her papa more.

"It's Great-Grandpa Pau!" the girl insisted. "Stop lying," Anaïs said, wrenching the notepad out of her hands.

A group of teenagers sat nearby with their music on full blast. One of the passengers asked them to turn it down, but they told him no, that if he didn't want to hear their music, he'd have to switch cabins. A wad of gum blew up into an immense bubble, like a globe, lingering beneath the unblinking, joyless gaze aimed at the passenger. A gaze belonging to a fish. But Anaïs didn't have room for any more thoughts. And the noise of the wheels on the track in her ears and the jolts of her head against the glass and Foix describing her drawing again, muttering with her nose pressed against the window: "It's Great-Grandpa Pau."

A voice announced the breakdown. All passengers were to exit the train. At Vilafranca Station, she held on tight to Foix's hand, carrying the bag of Foix's dirty clothes in her other hand. A wide street lined with shuttered wine cellars unfolded beneath a grey sky, an abandoned vineyard in the background. The bad news tormented her senses, like an all-but-imminent death. She remembered the young people with their *maquineo* on full blast, how there was no earning their respect, the giant bubble of gum beneath two fish eyes. The ghost of Grandpa Pau in Foix's drawing and the threat looming over the landscape paralysed her legs on that sleepy Sunday street — its own kind of breakdown.

He hit the gas and left the truck trailing behind him.

Sundays weren't usually this slow, but the national road was always packed. And how much worse would it get if the road were surrounded by more, even larger warehouses? Jan's stomach began to growl as he thought about it. He was close to Vilafranca now, but he kept cursing. That fucking train.

The fucking breakdowns on that fucking train. Poor Anaïs. Poor little Foix. A family lunch awaited them at Vilarer. He was so hungry that he rummaged through the storage compartment in the car door in case any old scraps of junk food were lying around. Nothing there, just the torn wrapper from the condom he'd used the night before at the lookout point with Samira. And there was no getting ahead on that damned highway.

He drove up to the train station after crossing the listless town; Sundays were always sleepy there. He saw Anaïs and Foix, their bags on the ground as they awaited rescue. He pulled to a stop right beside them. Foix ran up to him, squealing with joy and holding her pink backpack up with her arms so it wouldn't slide down her little body. He gave her a piggy-back ride, and she burst out laughing. Give *me* some of that joy, would you? Anaïs looked exhausted, like she hadn't had the best day. Maybe he shouldn't say anything right now. And without talking much at all, off they went to Vilarer.

They walked into their grandparents' empty house, and Jan thought it smelled the same as always. It was lucky that their father had held onto everything in the country. Not only was it good for get-togethers, but it had the same aroma from before Grandma Selma had been widowed, from before she herself had died.

The shade the fig tree cast on the porch was of no use on

a cloudy day like that. Jan remembered how, in a poem, Joan Vinyoli had said that porches were "hideaways for words." A pile of almonds lay on the table. Nobody had touched them but it was nice enough that someone had bothered to gather them at all. The staircase to the rooftop had no handrail, and one of the steps — not even a step anymore, just a plank of rotten wood — wobbled underfoot. And there were no animals in the barn, just tools and abandoned equipment. Jan climbed up to the roof to check if he'd forgotten any T-shirts on the clotheslines up there; he wouldn't want to leave their fates to the wind. Half the town's rooftops, dotted with chimneys, stretched as far as he could see. And at the end of town, he saw the green steeple of the belltower, unusually dull that autumn midday.

The others were getting lunch ready. Jan came down from the roof and put one last glass on the table, which seemed larger now. Some people had died, others were separating, and still others were migrating. He knew Aunt Empar would judge everyone, and that Uncle Xavier would support the logistics centre. But Jan had to keep his cool. At least over lunch. That's what their father, and especially Foix, deserved. And Anaïs, what about her? Cousin Jaume arrived. Hi, Jan. Hello, Jaume. How are classes going? Oh, they're going. Who knew what Jaume was doing at university? Cousin Víctor arrived. Hello, Víctor. Víctor barely uttered a word or lifted his gaze from the little screen he cradled in his hands.

"And what will you do now, *nena*, without a man by your side?" Empar prodded.

"I have so many plans, I don't even know where to start, Auntie," Anaïs replied.

Salads were passed down the table as the clamour grew louder. Wine bottles went this way and that. Remarks struck like matches for an inevitable fire. It had been three months since the grape harvest, and they recalled how the xarel·lo grape had been affected by disease. How could it be, that much rot, all that ashy fruit? What had gone wrong? Who had failed? Father laid out his excuses. It was quite enough that he was dealing with the fields at all, when that wasn't the work he actually lived off! Uncle Xavier said that it was no big deal, and for Magí not to sweat it since the vineyard wouldn't turn a profit whether the grapes were good or bad. Jan said that maybe it was the ploughing, the pruning, inadequate treatment, the drought, or maybe climate change. Empar asked who wanted spaghetti. Jaume questioned everything. Víctor was glued to his phone. But Anaïs spoke clearly:

"Only Grandpa Pau would know what went wrong. It's too much of a drag, going to the vineyard, isn't it, Dad?"

While the plates were emptied of pasta, Jan thought about how everything was getting muddled up. There was a tense, imaginary thread holding everyone's gazes, weaving through half-empty bottles and scraped platters. He knew that Uncle Xavier would be in favour of the compulsory purchase. A compulsory purchase in favour of grey warehouses. The Logistics Centre would swallow up vineyards, partitions, paths and dry-stone huts in its cement. He'd be in favour of it because keeping the land was no longer profitable. It was all the same to him if Jan and Anaïs said that the market was to blame for the poor grape prices — it wasn't the land's fault. It was all the same if they said that maybe this green and red landscape needn't be destroyed. Or if they said that agricultural plots could survive under a different economic model. Wine loosened their tongues. Muscatel raised their voices. Jaume conceded. Maybe he'd found their words nice enough. And Aunt Empar noted that the flan was scrumptious, wasn't it? Uncle Xavier said that the compulsory purchase was fine. Anaïs said that it wasn't fine at all. And that a citizen's platform was trying to stop the project.

"They're just a couple of buffoons."

"Don't say that, Uncle Xavier."

Anaïs accused him of having no memory, no feelings, no blood. Uncle Xavier said it wasn't about that, but rather about progress. And she said that his progress would wash away every living colour. Her father complained that he was being forced to sell, that they were seizing Llobeta Vineyard from him unjustly, against his will. Anaïs was no longer confronting her uncle, but her father, saying that he couldn't accept payment, that to accept any compensation would be to sell out Grandpa Pau's memory and that she'd never forgive him. And then Jan didn't know which way to turn. Silence weighed down on the table, and on everyone, like a slab of stone, their jaws hanging open in awe. The flan had been gobbled up. Wine glasses froze mid-air, paralysed.

"What in the world are you talking about my child? If I don't take the money, they'll take my land anyway," Magí said.

"You can't do it. Have some dignity."

"Anaïs… Grandpa Pau is dead. Times have changed," said her father.

"You can't take the money."

Foix ate her flan with no spoon, slurping it up from her plate. Jan thought that if he'd noticed earlier, he would have either told her to eat it properly or laughed along. Foix jumped into the conversation all on her own.

"Grandpa Pau is alive!" Foix cried. Víctor looked up from his phone, perplexed, bubbles tapering in the flutes of cava.

"Foix. Again?" Anaïs said.

"It was him. I promise, Mama, it was him!"

"Go to the garage and come back once you've thought about what you've said," Anaïs ordered.

Jan's eyes followed the girl as she walked under the weight

of everyone's uncomfortable stares, a little stuffed bear under her arm, her ponytail bouncing in her Hello Kitty scrunchie as she grew distant among the fig leaves. With just one look, their father communicated to Anaïs that Foix was just a child. Anaïs got up and said, "You can't take the money." She left the porch, and the house too, and started up the road. Their father followed her, but she was walking very quickly, up the road to Quatrecases. Jan watched them from the doorway for a while. The road was empty and the nearby houses gave off the scent of firewood. And he went back to the porch. A motorcycle whizzing by at full speed shook the metal door, and the lizards slipped into the cracks in the entryway. The metal door echoed across the entire porch and an almond fell from the pile, rolling down to the dirt between the squashed figs and yellowing leaves that were also falling — the breeze exposing the unused farm equipment as the old sheet covers fluttered in the wind.

The situation left him feeling uncomfortable. He too wanted to flee from that gathering. He wanted to see Samira again, because only she would tell him he was right about everything, and only she could hold the silence. He wanted to go back to the lookout point by the chapel. He wanted the silence to be eclipsed by the opaque waters in Foix Swamp, by the unkempt vineyards and bewildering fog, for it to be filled with beer cans and cigarettes. He wanted to go there with her, like always, so that they could both pretend the silence didn't belong to them. That their love wasn't really there, that it was all just pleasure and joy and flesh. That the family he hated was simply far away.

There was Jan, the square classroom, its white walls and loud children. There was Samira close by, so close he could pass her notes. There was Samira's curly hair, tidier now than on Saturday after picking grapes. And her white T-shirt and those white bike shorts against her tan skin. There was his teacher, who encouraged him to raise his hand if anything applied to him. If you did this or that during the break, raise your hand. Which one of you clever children can tell me this? Raise your hand. There were his tracksuit shorts, sweat-soaked from sitting, and his wrinkly elbow on the desk, one fist sinking into his cheek, his other hand raised each time he felt called on.

There was his father, along with Grandpa Pau and Uncle Xavier, who were harvesting grapes a mile away from school. Over where he could be playing in the dry-stone hut, the trailer giving off its familiar scent, if it weren't for him having to sit through class. There was Samira's father, whom they'd hired. And Anaïs, who was already grown up because she'd turned twenty and had a business card with her telephone number on it saying she was a graphic designer, and she could help out because she worked from home and could move her schedule around however she liked. And his arms crossed beneath the desk, his eyes resting on Samira's skin as he yearned for Saturday to arrive, with a pressing desire to peel himself out of that chair, so he could go out to the vineyard. There was Mohamed, who would bring Samira over with him on Saturday so they could play. There was his little cousin Jaume in Aunt Empar's arms, meaning that she couldn't do much but walk around, and Grandma Selma's back, meaning that she was in no condition to work all that much either.

There was "The Harvest" written on the chalkboard in big

letters, and the smell of must and damp earth, not noticeable in the classroom. And above everything else, chalked in cursive, "Monday, September 15th, 1986." There was his teacher again, defining tendril, bunch, turnrow, must, graft, plough, wheel hoe, furrow and pedicel. There was the phrase "I'm borred" written in the note that Jan threw at Samira's feet after catching her attention with a pssst. And "I found somthing secret in the shed" in the note Samira threw back. "Wil you show me?" And Samira, giving a thumbs up to match her mischievous smile. There was the teacher again, defining graft, pedicel, bunch, turnrow, tendril, wheel hoe, plough, furrow and must. And the eraser clearing it all away in a flash — like the wind.

There was each and every angle, lit up in the sky blue of Saturday. And Samira on one side of the grapevine, him on the other, the two of them leaving it bare, immaculately empty, like back at the beach when they'd dig holes in the sand, fill up their buckets, bury each other. There were the bunches of grapes that would fall, snip by snip, into the bucket, plop, plop, plop. And their hands combing through the multitude of vine leaves, between the powdery green and the grey cobwebs, the white spider and the bright greenfly. There was the overflowing bucket, and Jan calling out to the older folks, their heads bobbing up along the walkways, wanting to know what was going on and how they could help: Grandpa, Dad, Uncle, Anaïs, friends of the family and Mohamed. There were Grandpa Pau's shoulders, carrying the overflowing bucket after hoisting it up by both handles. There was the look on Jan's face, and Grandpa Pau's sheer strength, honed over the years. There was his grandfather's worn shirt, dirty from the endless buckets, the grapes and the green of the leaves that brushed his back when he cleared the vines. And him shouting, "Goddammit! You little devils, don't fill 'em up so much next time, I'm getting old." And the brrrrruuuum sound when he'd unload all the grapes in the trailer at the same time. There was the empty bucket, ready to be filled again. And the shears climbing up and down in the background, the flies dancing eagerly in the leftover must.

There was Jan, gripping the trailer's tow ball, Anaïs by his side and Samira by hers. And the tractor in high gear beneath his father's calloused hands, the gigantic wheels meeting the asphalt. There were hands blackened by the harvest and legs stained purple by a mixture of must and grape-leaf dust. And the landscape, which swelled as the vineyard receded into the background, reducing everybody to a mottle of specks against the various shades of summer. There was the engine and the wind, which would've kept them from hearing his father if he'd been scolding them for eating grapes from the bucket. There was Grandpa Pau, who would've said, "Goddammit! You little devils, stop eating up the harvest, that's a pound less we'll sell."

There was the candy in the pocket of the woman supervising the grapes. And the race towards her to ask for some, Samira and the kids from the other tractors behind him, everyone wanting sweets and wanting them now. There was the cooperative cellar and the smell it gave off at that time of year, a mix of damp earth crusted onto gigantic wheels, must rising up from the cellar itself, freshly pressed grapes and dirt from the vineyard impregnating their clothes. There was his father's slow and bulky manoeuvring to weigh the tractor's haul. And the gear stick in neutral. And the woman at the scales, with her green plastic boots and candy in her pockets, who came straight over to weigh the grapes and see if they were acceptable or not. There was the line, slowly growing longer, of tractors dragging the trailers overflowing with white grapes.

There were all the children there alongside him, running between the people in the wine cellar and screaming at the tops of their lungs. There was the main event, just about to start, and the race toward the chute, with Samira and the others behind him, but he ran faster than them all because being up front meant he'd get a better look. There was his father, who had already left the scales, backing up to attach the trailer to the chute. There was the opening that older folks said was dangerous and the inside of the co-op cellar, with metal-grate stairs and dirt floors spread out at their feet. And Anaïs — who was making it look like she'd come closer to watch over them but seemed to be enjoying it just as much as they were — told them how their ancestors from Vilarer had built it with their own hands because they could no longer stand being poor. And Samira, who took advantage of the moment to ask how much Anaïs earned picking grapes. There was Jan looking at Samira's gaping mouth, her chin sticking out, as Anaïs explained that no, she didn't earn a thing, that no one in her family did and that Samira would understand when she was older.

There was his father saying, "You little devils, don't lean so far forward," and then Jan taking the tiniest step back from the railing. There was the trailer, which was beginning to tilt and release its first bunches of grapes, little by little before the booming fall. There was the show, which had already begun, and Jan staring at it, entranced like his sister, although she was twenty years old. There were all the grapes, the toiling hours of collecting them and the single instant in which they all fell downward, crushed beneath the metal bars.

There were walls made of stone and brick, and the large arched windows above the muck below. There was the hose a man was using to wash down his sticky trailer. And the pile of pedicels at the back door, out in the open air like it didn't matter, giving off their usual smell, and no one would fuss over the pile, nor all the other things that couldn't be used to make wine. There was the tow ball on the trailer again and the wind and the fields as far as the eye could see — dirt paths and stone partitions, twisting and turning. There was Llobeta Vineyard and all the other grown-ups, visored hats, tangled hair, aching backs, shoes with holes in them, and the oppressive sun. In the distance, the white shed kept Samira's secret inside — and it was high time she told him what it was.

There were the Twin Mountains, which drew the sun ever closer. There was the race towards the shed, towering like a crown in the middle of the vineyard, and the far-off harvesters on the other side. There was Samira and him, no one else. And Jan giving the wooden door a shove and two frightened lizards scuttling between the dry stones all over again. There were the tools, the dirt and grime, the old junk. And a single piece of furniture, decaying and tilting from a missing leg. There was a drawer and, within it, a cardboard box. There was Samira's gaze, attentive and electric. There was the box's lid, and "Summer of 1986" scribbled on it in blue ink. And tools strewn about the dirt floor where they sat and opened the mysterious box. There were cardboard compartments. In each one, ceramic pieces in different shades of brown with wavy patterns and the occasional handle, and a note with the name of one of Grandfather Pau's vineyards. There were pieces from the compartment labelled "Llobeta," which Samira said had been found right there, under their feet. There was Samira's euphoric curiosity and Jan's silence. And Samira's voice, hoarse and parched, in search of an accomplice and a storybook adventure.

"Who do you think collected all of these?" she asked.

"I don't know, I don't really care…" he said impatiently, looking towards the door.

"What do you think they wanted with all this?" she wondered, fretting.

"Should we hunt for lizards?" he asked, grabbing a glass jar.

There was the colour of the sky, transforming. And the other side of the vineyard where Anaïs stood, calling over to them, waving her arms up and down so they could see her better. She shouted, "Come on, let's go, let's go." And there were Anaïs's dirty shears too, waving up and down. She hardly ever went anywhere without them.

THE DRAWING

The swallows, which no longer chirped under the old balconies, sat on the distant power lines like parched furrows. And the stench of barns, of crops, of humidity wafting through the night, and the echoes of tractors, and the murmur of the recent harvest — marking the town's continued survival — loomed over the skirt of the Twin Mountains as if for the last time. Anaïs felt like she was capable of anything that might put a stop to that project. When she saw the Twin Mountains, the Talaia summit peeking through in the distance, she felt certain that this land could simply never be smeared with concrete. The mountain had always sustained the fields below, pulling the dirt roads up its sides, lending its name to the vineyards, guarding its farmers from the sun. In her grandparents' and great-grandparents' photo albums, the valley always appeared crowned by the Twin Mountains, no matter the angle. No, there was no way. The mountain existed *because* there was a plain. No one would dare cut off its lower limb.

She felt like fleeing from that family lunch gathering, like being alone, but when she got to the Llobeta Vineyard, she saw an old man exiting the stone hut. That shed, which had always looked like an igloo to her, albeit one made of dry stone, poked through the almond trees lining the partition around her father's vineyard. What was that stranger doing there? What could he possibly be looking for? Why would anyone want to surround themselves with old knick-knacks, dust and cobwebs? What could he want with those old tools that Grandpa Pau had kept but that nobody used anymore? He looked familiar. She pulled her notebook out of her bag and hastily leafed through it until she found Foix's drawing. He wore a beret and espadrilles, like the man in the picture. So not only was he plotting something in the hut, but he was also bothering her daughter. She wouldn't let her ride her bike on her own anymore, she always went too far. "Beat it!" she hollered. The mountain echoed her cry, and in a fleeting rush a couple of birds darted from the stone partition to take refuge in the carob tree. She saw the man turn his head slowly, startled by her cry. When she noticed that his back was hunched and that he had a limp, she stopped frowning and gulped saliva down her raw throat. She could tell that the man was looking her in the eye, but he didn't say a word. He just lowered his head and went on his way. She stood there, paralysed in the turnrow, watching that stranger's shadow grow smaller as he scurried down the Pi de Llobets path, weaving between the vines, midrows and almond and olive groves. "Get out of here! I don't want to see you around here anymore! Keep your hands off my grandfather's things! And don't you dare touch my daughter!"

"Who are you yelling at, Anaïs?" her father asked, panting. He'd been running after her, trying to catch up. "A thief," she said, her eyes peeled on the stranger who was winding away into the distance. "But there's no one here, Anaïs..." he said. She kept yelling anyway — her cries spreading out like the shadows that dappled every nook and cranny of the plain at dusk. What kind of a person would even think of going into her shed, talking to her daughter, treading her grandfather's land without permission? But he was nobody — not a politician, not the machines that wrecked the vines, not her father who had come to spy on her, not the immense carob tree where she'd build forts as a child, peering out at the crest and slope, perched among the branches. And suddenly the carob deserved a few good kicks.

And when she started kicking, her father steadied her in his arms. And she pulled back from him and from the tree, burying her face in her hands. But her fingers couldn't hide the streaming tears. With her back to the tree, she looked out at the vineyard.

That autumn was nothing like the others. The wind had gathered too many leaves beneath the vines. The shoots and buds should have been pruned in the spring, like her grandfather used to do, but her father had forgotten to. The neglect was all on him. He had dishonoured her grandfather's memory. She felt his hand on her shoulder, but she drew back and stormed out to where the vines began. As she touched the desiccated leaves, which absorbed the tears on her fingers, she understood why the grapes hadn't been good that year: her father hadn't tended the vines in the spring, he hadn't tended to the grey spots, to the parasites, the sporangia, the aeration… or used the right products required to avoid disease. He was in charge of the vineyard and hadn't done the job. He had dishonoured her grandfather, and she reminded him of that, livid as the imminent sunset, a soaked handkerchief in hand. Had he forgotten the advice that her grandfather had passed down to them? Did he want to be like the folks who owned the next vineyard over, who didn't even harvest their grapes anymore? As her cries peaked, he drew back. But she didn't stop, her throat cracking like bone-dry earth as she yelled, her gaze darting from him to the vines and back. Would he prune the vines as he was supposed to this winter? Or would he just pile up a few poorly cut vines on the forgotten path that led to the Holy Mary of Foix church?

She spoke of her grandfather's memory.

The sun had disappeared behind the imposing mountain, the mountain that shielded the plain and guarded it from the gusts now making a whirlwind of her hair, between her sobs, the handkerchief at her nose, her tired eyes piercing the rows of grapevine canes. Her father sat beneath the carob tree, enduring the tirade. He let a devastating silence take over the space between them. She spoke of her grandfather, his indefatigable tractor, his dirt-caked hands on the steering wheel, his wrinkled forehead, black beret, navy blue espadrilles, grey scarf, dark brown trousers, his faded shirt tied haphazardly around his weary shoulders on the last days of the harvest. He had scolded her, thirty years ago, for eating grapes from the trailer, grapes that were meant to be sold. He'd scolded her instead of yelling at the big cava producers who were cheapening the vine by slashing their prices to make more off their exported bottles, sinking the grapevines under, little by little, making a mockery of the men who worked on dirt roads under the harsh sun, the leaves decked in filth and spiders, the shears snipping at bare branches. They scoffed at those who got up early like him, at the red plain on humid autumn evenings, the verdant plain of glorious summers.

Sat on the ground beneath the carob tree, she turned everything over in her head as she drew spirals in the earth with a twig. Their industry was doomed, but people didn't care. And the Logistics Centre was coming like a prophesied meteor. And how could her father say that it was no big deal now that her grandfather was dead, that the times had changed. How could he, if only the dignity of his memory could save them?

Her father sat beside her and appeared to be considering her string of accusations. The barking in the distance came to a lingering pause. The dirt turnrows punctuated with twigs, carobs, stones. And Anaïs insisted that he couldn't take the money, that he couldn't sell the vineyard, that he would have to let it be seized from him before he dishonoured her grandfather. Okay, I won't sell it. He said it just like that, decisively. Even if they take it from me, he added. And Anaïs let out a sigh of relief under the heavy pumpkin moon. She had not felt at peace like that since she'd separated from Foix's father a few months back, at the age of forty.

Now they just had to put a stop to the Logistics Centre's construction plans, she said. That wasn't in either of their hands, he replied. And she said that wasn't true and swore to him that no one would dare lay a finger on this place, he could rest assured.

THE BURIAL

The tolling of the funeral bells replaced the rumble of tractors on that weekday morning in October of 1987, when all the town's farmers left their olive groves behind to make their way to the church and cemetery. Anaïs had turned twenty-one and was reflecting — in a deep, foggy way — about death and the turn of the seasons. The streets of Vilarer began to absorb the circumspection of winter, while each day seemed to merely chip away at the long expanse of night, daily motions once again became routine, the harvest faded into the distance and the tangle of scents grew mild. Almonds piled up on the chilly patios to be shelled in bulk. Grandpa Pau, though, was no longer there. The bars were emptying out as the drink and coffee orders dwindled. And young people were listing a whole host of feasible goals for a fairly predictable year ahead. But that day Anaïs left with her sunglasses on, while a black ribbon that had been pinned to the flag on the town hall balcony waved in the humid air.

Bodies clothed in sombre hues had flooded carrer Francesc Macià at the same pace as they'd filled the church to the brim. Anaïs had wanted to be just another face in the crowd, but she was the deceased's eldest grandchild. She would have liked a terrible tempest to move in, a cruel hailstorm to dispel that sea of fools, all of them strangers. For while the Vilarer belltower kept its hold on the black and silent multitude, the silence, the fresh air and the intermittent tolling of the solemn bells allowed some of them to melt into feelings of freedom within the overwhelming sadness that moment demanded. No one would criticise them for being too loud or dressing bizarrely. No one would criticise them for not uttering a word or for making a sour face. No one would find any of it strange, but some came to mourn or give their condolences, and some showed up merely to show up, free of excuses old and new, to join in on that collective feeling, that ritual offering the space to grieve any old loss at all.

Seated near the front by the plume of candle smoke, Anaïs caught sight of the coffin coming down the aisle, and she imagined her grandfather Pau slowly rising from it, maybe propping it open or walking through it. He'd be wearing a beret and navy-blue espadrilles and would set off towards the vineyard on foot. But then she saw Grandma Selma in the front row, watching that flower-covered coffin draw closer and closer. Her eyes looked tired. For a moment, she thought that maybe her grandmother only wanted him out of that box so that the fields wouldn't go untended, so the grapevines wouldn't darken with the passing of each sunset or turn into raisins when grazed by the dust kicked up by the mistral winds. Sure, because it was no coincidence that he'd died by falling from a broken olive tree branch during the harvest. And the whole tree went down with him, rotten as it already was inside. And surely she'd be pleading with him, reproaching him for having never got up from the table after they both came back from the vineyard, and for always expecting her to take care of the house and the children as well as the animals and the land. Or maybe she'd be full of praise for him now that he was no longer around, and surely she'd be praying to her saints and God and the Virgin Mary, believing them to be with her. She saw that, contemplative before the smoke and incense and with visible melancholy for a marriage that had soured years beforehand, her grandmother was staring at something somewhere that wasn't the aisle. A man, but he wasn't Grandpa Pau. He was lingering in the corner of the chapel. Dressed in black, his head bowed — a shadow of guilt, condolence and hope traced the presence of that man whom Grandma Selma appeared surprised to see. She seemed totally absorbed. Anaïs imagined a shiver running down the length of her grandmother's body, from the crown of her mantilla to the bottom of her feet. And what about him? Who was he, the man in the corner of the chapel, staring at the ground, who seemed to share, down to the very last detail, in the rawness that lingered among the attendees?

Anaïs didn't take off her sunglasses once that day. With them on, she protected herself from the discomfort of getting out of the hearse and meeting the wave of people on the street, of receiving the perfunctory condolences of strangers, of sitting through a sermon that refused to end. And when she ran into the friends her grandfather used to play cards with, who were at a loss for words near the front door of the café, their eyes fixed on the church steps, and when she felt a profound hatred for the garish, gossipy ladies who didn't even know who it was they were supposed to offer their condolences to, she felt the immature impulse to take off running.

She stared more often at the floor than at the ceremony. One persistent thought stood apart from the rest: the firm wish that everyone would simply leave. That the rows, all lined up and cold like grapevines tied back in February, would simply disappear. That the crowd in the cemetery would vanish into thin air and leave her alone with her family. But maybe everyone leaving wouldn't change a thing. Besides her grandfather, many other things had gone too, because the time of living off the land alone had ended, and her father wouldn't do as good a job, of course not, and she felt that something would change from there on out. And she had already turned twenty-one and was reflecting — in a deep, foggy way — about death and the turn of the seasons. She felt, with a full, young and intense sense of self, that part of her had evaporated like water off the forgotten bunches of grapes.

THE PILLOW

She remembered all of it, unsure if she was reminiscing out of
spite, guilt or both. She'd begun 2007 with plenty of goals. And
she toyed with each one in bed, realising that her separation had
given her a lot more time to think. She had to admit that she,
too, had abandoned the vineyard years ago. What good would
saving the vineyard have been if it could no longer turn a profit?
What would she have done with it if she *had* saved it, given that
she didn't work the land? Since her grandfather's passing, they'd
brought flowers to the cemetery every All Saints' Day, but no
one had kept vigil over the magnificent earth he'd left behind.

So many years had passed... And her father had resigned
himself to tending the crops in his little spare time. She couldn't
blame him. She couldn't, the way she had that December afternoon as the sun set over Llobeta Vineyard. Since he actually
made a living from working at the co-op store, and no one was
paying any more per pound of grapes despite the rising costs
of living. There was no way he could be a winemaker alone, not
without another job. And as if that weren't enough, every September
he'd live in fear of being fined for having grape-pickers working
without a contract, now that the police had started inspecting
the grounds. Had they gone mad? How were they supposed to
hire the neighbours and family who were just there to help out?
How could any of it turn a profit? No, there was no way she
could hold a grudge against him. She knew that *other* people
were guilty, that really they were the same people who didn't
pay enough for the grapes, the same ones who constructed giant
concrete facilities without a care for those who worked the land.

She missed those Septembers.

Uncle Xavier and Aunt Empar had stopped picking grapes
now that Grandpa Pau was no longer around to make them.

They'd been swept away by their routines, children, jobs, a maddening world that wouldn't stop turning, pulling them one way then the other. She, too, could toss and turn in bed, which now seemed large and plush, all she liked. And Jaume and Víctor had been raised barely learning to harvest at all. And she'd look back and put herself in her little cousins' shoes, picturing her own childhood with such an immense void. How would Jan's childhood have been without the harvests? And Samira's? She realised that her father had been deserted, and now he had to hire Mohamed to tend the vines, and a lot of other people too, because otherwise they'd fine him — plus, the family had more important things to do than picking grapes, and the neighbours who could help out were few and far between.

She thought of her grandmother.

Grandma Selma was named after an abandoned town. Selma had a belltower with warm-toned shingles, and its population had dwindled because it was too far from the new highway that severed the Montmell mountain range in two. Even abandoned, it was a lovely town, and when she'd make the trek there, lost in the middle of it all, she felt at such peace, knowing that it was a privilege to be the granddaughter of someone who'd borne the same name. Grandma Selma had grown old, and her uncle and father had had to take care of her because she'd carried them in her womb and, as the years passed, she could barely walk or talk, like a tree, and the breeze on the porch would part her white bangs as her sons would spoon-feed her purée. And when she died of old age everyone returned to the church and then the cemetery.

Death made her think of her mother.

There'd been unexpected complications during Jan's birth, but her mother had lived long enough to teach her to love the land and love her neighbour. The cemetery had become almost a home to her. Her mother was there. She held onto everything she'd learned from both her mother and grandmother. She'd hold onto it always, and pass it on to Foix. What she no longer had was their voices, since their bodies were buried under cement. And anything lying under cement would never come back. Death was an absolute. Destruction, however, was a battle with winners and losers.

She was no better than anyone else. She designed wine-bottle labels, but that had little to do with the land. She'd built a place for herself at the top of carrer de Dalt, and now she stared at the ceiling with her head resting on the pillow. She'd set up a design studio in her dining room. She'd designed every morning and afternoon, she'd married and built a life far removed from the land. And when Foix was born she'd stopped having time for herself. And she'd thought about her mother a lot when she gave birth, but she was gone. And Foix's father had let go of any and all romance the day after they got married. And the house had two floors, and the garden was big, and the road to Quatrecases was long, and the sea was immense on the horizon.

She was only truly happy when she'd touch up wine labels on her computer screen.

Jan had grown up. Once he reached adolescence, he started missing school, not because of the harvest but because he was smoking pot, and then he went to university where he studied literature because he liked poetry and books. And he was in love with Samira, who'd studied anthropology because she liked observing things and gathering answers. They were friends who cared for each other, but their relationship came and went. They were the same but different. Jan never talked to her about it much, but Anaïs knew it because she was like the mother he'd never had.

Jaume and Víctor were growing up and glued to their video

games. They studied and worked summers — anything but farming — to pay for their whims, and they also smoked weed and were learning about life. To them, the vineyard was something of a forlorn past, something that belonged to the grandfather they didn't remember, the grandmother they'd only met when she was already out of it, when they were very young indeed.

Her father hired workers so he wouldn't be fined. No one else helped out because it was no longer customary. Her poor father, he didn't even have the time to ask himself what had happened, or why it was that he got paid so little for his grapes, so little for those fields of green rows under the beating sun that he might as well have thrown in the towel. And whenever he did stop to ask himself why things were that way, it was only to say that as long as the co-op kept selling most of its product to the large cava exporters, he'd be paid a pittance for his grapes.

It was true. She, too, had abandoned the vineyard that would now be ripped up then buried. And that's why she'd finally had to switch off the bedside light and shut her eyes, think lovely thoughts and fall asleep so she could wake up in the small hours and trim Llobeta Vineyard, though she'd never done it before. She had to do it now that it was January, yes, like her grandfather had done — before the grapevines started to wake, producing their sap so they could grow once more.

She woke up at four, planted a kiss on Foix's forehead and let her stay in bed. She took some shears from the garage and revved up the engine. She wore a raincoat and wrapped a scarf all the way up to her nose, like Grandpa Pau would do as he sat atop the tractor at the crack of dawn, back in the day. It was still dark, but she trusted the moon and had a headlamp in her pocket.

She swiftly trimmed branch after branch so she'd be on time to take Foix to school. Cut in the dark, the naked branches fell to the ground — snip, snap, snip, snap — one over the other until the shy morning light began to clear up the sky and Anaïs gathered up the sticks into a single pile.

She pruned for days. First at dawn, since she had other work needing her attention during the day, what with her daughter and the wine labels. But then it took over. She abandoned her design work, but it didn't matter. This is more important, she thought. It's okay if Foix is alone for a little while. It's okay if my father and Jan come and spy on me, if they're taken aback by my new way of doing things, if they say I'm just a bit obsessed.

When she'd finished pruning, she started looking for pieces of ancient pottery between the rows of vines, sifting through the humid earth that'd camouflaged them. Her old, secret hobby would come in handy now. She could piece the Phoenician jugs back together so they'd have to put a stop to the logistics complex in the hope of finding ancient ruins. She'd bend down to rummage through the rows, find little bits and pieces, and pick them up. The years of ploughing and tilling had started to break them up, bringing them to the surface. She was convinced that under the earth lay a discovery that would shatter everything people thought they knew. Something that would prove that the Penedès vineyards dated much further back than people thought. And it would be such a staggering discovery that there'd be no way the construction would ever begin, because historians, lawyers, mayors, councillors and general directors of culture would have no choice but to bring them to grinding halt.

ELISA

She left the report half-finished and got up from her desk, concentrating on holding in her pee. Elisa's ash-blonde hair, now peppered with grey, no longer hid that she was in her fifties. She looked at herself in the mirror. Her austere expression tended to scare off her colleagues. She knew she commanded respect, that there was no need to dye her hair, wear makeup, nothing. No jewels, no lively colours. But she also knew that she was far from subdued. No one would ever hear her raise her voice, but everyone stood back when she passed by, naturally — perhaps because they felt intimidated, or perhaps because they simply admired her experience, firmness and elegance. And she was proud of it. Her wrinkles did even less to disguise her fifty years. Her bare skin was pale, though she sported a somewhat malevolent smile and green eyes that were clearly full of strength — and longed for a return to happiness.

Elisa left the bathroom and noticed that the waiting room sounded like a madhouse. And she was not in the mood. Noise wasn't allowed on the third-floor offices of the county's social services building. She whispered in the ear of the secretary, who said, "Shhh," and everyone lowered their voices. Then she shut herself up in her office. She'd requested that the secretary say that she wasn't around if anyone asked for her; everyone could wait. She ran the risk of seeming uncongenial, but it was only that she wanted to respect her own time. And when she heard the door shut behind her, she kept still for a second, staring at the computer screen with her fingers hovering over the keyboard, welcoming the solitude behind the closed door. She took a deep breath and looked at the balcony of her outdated office. The pigeons' balcony, she'd call it, with its railing covered in bird shit. The balcony overlooked a dead-end street, lacking any sense of the wider landscape of the town of El Vendrell. And she went right back to writing her report, picking up where she left off, to keep from thinking of anything else.

On an early Thursday morning in January, most of the staff had gone out for breakfast. An anonymous call bounced from phone to phone until someone finally picked up and transferred the call to her on that cold winter morning, with its drowsy air and ruffled pigeons on the balcony. It was Jordi, the social worker from the medical centre. He wanted to speak with her. He went quiet, not knowing where to start. He said that they were dealing with an unusual case. A man had set up a doctor's appointment, saying he was quite worried about his forty-year-old daughter, the mother of a minor, and asked what he could do if she refused to get psychiatric help. But Jordi had a hard time laying the facts out clearly, and he grew more nervous because Elisa coldly demanded brevity — he had caught her doing something important. His voice cowering and indignant in equal measure, he told her that if she was pressed for time, he could explain it in an email. "Okay," she said, hanging up the phone in relief, but she didn't pick up where she'd left off. She put the yellow highlighter in the jar, the papers in the tray, threw on her coat and grabbed her purse as she walked out to have a coffee.

She hurried down the stairs, her heels announcing her every step. Some of her colleagues poked out of their offices, wanting to consult with her on different matters, while others passed her on the stairs, asking her to sign off on their documents. She brushed them away almost effortlessly. She wasn't worried about her reputation. She was Elisa, after all, a luminary in the field, an imposing professional, the top social worker in the Northern Region. Luckily, in the afternoon, when she left the office and her colleagues went to pick up their kids at school, she did freelance consulting work on social matters. No one dared probe what feelings hid inside her because her authority and second job protected her. She reached the main door and after saying goodbye to the concierge and putting up with whatever joke he'd tell, which made everyone but her laugh, she wrapped her scarf around her neck to face the prickling cold.

Despite the weather and the depression in the air, the town was waking up. She crossed the tiled square and moved into the bustling historic district, where leftover traces of Christmas adorned the streets and sales breathed new life into the shops. A pigeon was resting on a Star of Bethlehem and, on the bar terraces, people shooed those same filthy birds away whenever they approached.

Before arriving at the bar where she was a regular, she hung back in front of a watch-shop window. She saw her image in the glass. Hands in her coat pockets, eyes just above her scarf, gaze fleeting towards the watches in the display window. When she was younger, Mateu would hold her hands in his to ward off the cold. She had picked out the best watch in the shop for him before they'd married. And he had given her that scarf last winter, before leaving her for another woman. Like a rejected pigeon, she thought. Later on, she found out that he'd already been cheating on her when he'd given her that scarf. There was another woman, and she hadn't appeared out of nowhere. The day he'd given her the gift was etched in her memory, and she held onto that image to convince herself that cynicism knows no limits. Believing that everything was a lie made her worries disappear. Dirty dishrag, rejected pigeon, she repeated to herself. That had been the cruellest of lessons, which stayed with her in her every waking, every gesture, every call, every meeting, every coffee, every meal, every night: it was all a lie, and if each word, promise, or offer was fragile like the pieces of a watch, then she was free to judge anyone as deluded, free to believe in no one but herself, not even a little bit. And while all that crossed her mind, the saleswoman came out, perhaps surprised by how her eyes remained fixed on the watches, and asked if there was anything she needed. Elisa said thank you but that she didn't give gifts, and no one ever gave her any either, thanks again. And she went off walking towards the bar, pulling her coat tighter and peering from side to side over her scarf, the slow and bold step of her heels resounding against the tiled street.

The various people passing by as she smoked her Winston cigarette next to the heater on the bar terrace made her think of how life went on. She leafed through the newspaper. Some three-hundred people, brought together through a citizen's platform, had blocked a national highway, protesting a logistics centre that was supposed to be built further inland, in wine country, between the national road and the toll road that connected the two central roadways. She licked her fingertips and turned the pages, her eyes attentive. She read that only ten percent of marriages last a lifetime, that domestic violence cases were on the rise, mental illness and child malnutrition too, that the far right kept resurging in Europe, that the polar ice caps were melting, and that as of that month, January 2007, a great economic crisis loomed. A young couple walked by with what looked like a three-year-old boy in a stroller. She observed their three-sided dynamic as they passed through the square. The guy said, "You're a bitch" in Spanish and the girl swallowed down those words only to spit some right back, saying, "Leave me alone," and then the child cried, "Mamá, mamá, mamá!" through his tears. Those two are crazy, she thought, walking around and dealing with all that. But how would she and Mateu have handled the separation if they'd had kids? She spent every day demanding that separated parents, those who used their children as a battlefield, be civil to one another, preaching about how kids should be kept out of their parents' fights. She didn't know how she and Mateu would've managed. During her time of mourning she'd been free to break into tears at any time or place, to triple her tobacco consumption between her own four walls, to insult Mateu left and right each time she hung up the phone or left the house. She would've had to hold so much back in front of a child. And then she wondered, just for a moment, what if she hadn't hidden her feelings at all? Who would judge her? She was made of flesh and bone, just like every other person who visited her office, people laden with stories that would keep you up at night, the victims of moral judgements that she herself was in charge of sentencing. But Elisa refused to show weakness for a single moment. That thought flew past, like the wind that caused her to lose her page in the newspaper, like the smoke of her cigarette, the flickering flame from the outdoor heater. Who would have dared doubt her? She was flawless, an example to be followed, the top social worker in the Northern Region, feet firmly on the ground. She was Elisa, and she would never, ever, ever be like ordinary people.

SAMIRA

Samira: It snowed all week. There's an empty lot in front of my house that's completely white and the roof is all white, too, and some days I can't even open the door because of all the snow.

Jan: So you found a place...

Samira: Yeah, it's on the outskirts of Montreal. I'm rooming with some of the other researchers on fellowship. Can't complain!

Jan: Glad to hear it.

Samira: What's new with you?

Jan: Nothing much... Still haven't found a job. If only I'd got my teaching certificate or whatever you call it, I'd be a language arts teacher, but I didn't do it when I had the chance, and now look at me.

Samira: It's never too late...

Jan: I don't have the energy to go back... And I don't really know where I want to be, geographically or professionally.

Samira: Me neither! But why the hell should we? Why does everything need to be so clear cut? Do you even remember all that vocabulary from school? Is any place static, isolated, un-changing in time?

Jan: I know, I know. Things change... And the logistics centre will upend the world as we know it. I really don't know where I'm going in life... And Anaïs is losing it.

Samira: Anaïs?

Jan: She's obsessed. She's always working in the vineyard. All she does is tend the vines, and she says she'll stop the logistics centre from destroying it all.

Samira: Right... a rebellious woman who tends the grapes all on her own. Or a woman, alone, who is rebellious *and* tends the grapes.

Jan: I mean, she doesn't even go to the citizen's platform. She'd rather be out there on her own, and like I said, all that being alone has got her seeing things that aren't there...

Samira: Ah... going to the platform would be the normal way of doing things, right?

Jan: My dad's on the same page as me... He even talked to a doctor about her, but I wouldn't have gone that far... That might have been a bit much.

Samira: But what does normal even mean? How would your grandfather have taken all this stuff with the logistics centre? And your grandmother?

Jan: Beats me...

Samira: What's normal anyway? Us fucking in the car that night in December? You reading poetry? Me studying anthropology? Never laying a foot on a goddam plot of farmland? What's an imaginary friend? Or an online friendship, like this one? A friendship built on sexual fantasies, stories from childhood, our ideas about each other? What conditions normality? Where is it classified? What are we? Who are we? To what time do we belong? Don't you think the landscape could tell us everything about our culture while remaining neutral in terms of anything *we* might think?

Jan: Jesus, what a speech! You're calling me out for reading poetry but you anthropologists sure know how to preach…

Samira: You're stuck in your ways! Nothing like a lit major… I'm out!

Jan: Samira, wait, don't leave!

Samira: I've got people waiting on me for lunch, but what's up?

Jan: I have to tell you something.

Samira: What?

Jan: I miss you…

Samira: Look, Jan… Sometimes I tell people that where I'm from, we have vineyards, but also almond, carob and olive trees lined up along the partitions. They're historical markers for where properties start and end, relics of a distant past when people could live off what they sowed.

Jan: Why are you changing the subject?

Samira: And then people ask me why we can't all live off such fertile land. And I tell them that now there are only vineyards, and that the wine has to be sold abroad because we produce more than we consume, and that devalues the bottles of wine and the grapes and the land.

Jan: You're right… The platform's really only concerned with preserving the landscape…

Samira: But here we are, still buying wine from across the Atlantic at the grocery store.

Jan: …when what we really need to do is rethink our economic model.

Samira: Okay, now I miss you! Hahaha.

Jan: It's just that… I love you.

Samira: We're friends, Jan…

Jan: Friends?

Samira: I know how we both feel about one another, but we both also need to do our own thing!

Jan: We're already thirty…

Samira: Need I remind you that at age twenty-five I still had to hide the fact that I drank, smoke and ate ham from my parents?

THE HEARTH

The dark sky had taken over all too soon, threateningly, and it depressed her that night fell so early on those late-January afternoons. She put the key in the lock, her hand trembling. Foix was standing right up against the doorway, anxiously awaiting the moment when the door would open so she could run inside and up the stairs, so as not to miss another minute of her cartoons. How Anaïs, too, longed to sit on the couch, relaxing and warming up by her little girl's side.

Having swapped her own shoes for slippers, Anaïs realised that Foix was still wearing her outside shoes, which she had up on the couch, her eyes glued to the screen. Anaïs would've told her to take them off, that it was always the same with her, that that was enough, that she never helped out and that she didn't love her as much as she did her dad. But she didn't feel like getting worked up again. After all, she'd already separated from Foix's father and had scolded her for making up a ghost who'd really turned out to be a thief. She sat down next to her daughter, picked up the book of poems Jan had lent her and let out a weary sigh. She'd had to wash all of Foix's clothes, those that her bum of an ex had conveniently ignored. And she'd had to go and buy the school supplies announced in the Friday bulletin that he hadn't even glanced at when picking up their daughter. But it wasn't their daughter's fault at all, and as Anaïs caressed Foix's hair while she attentively watched TV, she was convinced she wouldn't let herself get angry. In fact, she'd simply put down her book, take off the girl's shoes, and bring over her knitted slippers. And she'd get the thickest slippers she had in the wardrobe, so not a wisp of cold could sneak past the colourful yarn to the skin underneath — skin that was also her skin. Why should her little girl shoulder any of the blame for the separation? Why should her little girl take the blame for that handful of powerful people who'd decided to turn the landscape around them into a cement fortress?

She left Foix sitting there, her feet tucked under the blanket as the lamp light glowed softly, and scurried down to the garden, a blanket over her shoulders. Outside, moving quickly in the cold, she grabbed a bundle of firewood from the entryway. She was just going back into the house when she paused in front of the garage. Her cracked bits of pottery were safer there than in the shed, where that strange man would've found them. That day she'd found a bunch of them in the vineyard furrows. The colour of the Phoenician amphoras blended into the shades of earth, which made finding them even more of a feat. Would she be able to put many of them back together? Would it draw the attention of historians, who might suspect that an ancient site lay buried underneath? Would a site like that halt the construction? Maybe it, too, would lead to the vineyard being uprooted, but that would still be better than a warehouse. All that and more was running through her mind as she stood in front of the garage door, and then she went in, pooling her sweater so that she could carry up a few of the ceramic pieces, and climbed back up the stairs with a bundle of firewood under one arm and the tip of her sweater in her other hand.

Her daughter was drawing, sprawled out on the couch with the TV on. A half-finished sketch for a new wine label demanded her attention from a dark corner in the dining room, where her desk had remained untouched for days now. She didn't have time to think about business. Her daughter, the fire, the pieces of pottery...work could wait. She unloaded the wood into the fireplace and put the pieces on the coffee table. Nothing felt so satisfyingly useful to her as lighting a fire, because this warmth and this hearth were more important than anything else. Outside, the world had gone crazy. Winter pricked her skin. And the logs caught fire.

The snapped grapevine trunks let off sparks against the stone and iron hearth. She brought her hands closer to let the flames soothe them. Foix got off the couch and joined her, and they looked at each other and smiled. Almost instantly, all of her work, Foix's father, the warehouse, the wagging tongues, and the whole town of Vilarer melted away. And she put a rug down so Foix wouldn't have to sit on the bare floor while they warmed their hands by the fire. Foix grabbed the drawing to show Anaïs, and this time she hadn't drawn the old man near the shed, but rather Anaïs, her all-seeing mother. She suddenly felt that all her day-to-day sacrifices were worth it, because taking Foix to school, picking her up, feeding her lunch, working, giving her a snack, taking her to drawing class and picking her up all over again was thanks enough. Even if no one really thanked her, not her dad, nor Jan nor her bum of an ex. And she thought that nothing was more useful than having lit the fire so that she and Foix might celebrate the flames.

Foix's father stood far beyond their world, their eyes hypnotised by the raging fire. The newspaper was quickest to disappear, like her mother, who'd been in a rush to die when she was only ten years old. Foix was seven and history would not repeat itself, because her mother had gone and left Jan, and Anaïs hadn't wanted any more children, as time was money for those living under the patriarchy. Now she was rid of Foix's father, an extinguished flame. The pieces of grapevine trunk in the fire would also turn to ash, and ash matched the colour of cement. You couldn't put a price on freedom. Her mother would have surely understood the separation and all her struggles, but her father and Jan weren't really getting it at all. Why would they? They're men. Aunt Empar was there, but the patriarchy flowed right out of her, through her gaze and voice. The logo design kept calling for her attention from a dark corner in the dining room, but the land was real, the land wasn't some sketch, some inky concoction, something thought up by some Bohemian, some madman, some wine-drunk alcoholic. It was everything, because why would any of it matter — that darkened study, that house, that town — if it weren't surrounded by a landscape that was theirs alone?

Anaïs picked up the pieces of pottery from the table and put them back together to show Foix. She explained to her that they were shards of jugs that dated back thousands of years, that of course they might look like a bunch of pebbles to her, but she had to understand that the years and the tractors, the ploughs and the milling equipment, had chipped away at them. She had to really understand that, because if she found some piece of pottery in the dirt, between the grapevines and trunks in Llobeta Vineyard, she had to pick it up and give it to her mother immediately. Foix asked her if it was like when they searched for seashells at the beach, and she said, "Yes, exactly."

VISIONS

He slammed down the snooze button.

He would've liked to get up. He would've printed copies of his résumé and handed them out all over El Vendrell and Vila-franca, ready to take any job where his degree didn't matter. But for several odd months, he'd felt the need to catch up on sleep. He still wasn't at his best. Maybe he was wasting time. Maybe a bleak future was around the corner. He had the room's darkness, the warmth of a thick comforter, the woollen blankets…blankets he'd abandon only for Samira. Not a single shaft of light came through the blinds. *Riiing!* The alarm clock blared a second time. He poked his arm out from under the comforter and shut off the clock with a slap. Then he curled up in his blanket den.

Suddenly a cruel light poured over all four walls as he stretched out his arm and pried the blinds open. He could see the alarm clock on the bedside table with a single, open eye: it was getting too late to make it out to the cities, and that Wednesday would weigh on his shoulders much like any other that January. His father would say his piece about him not waking up on time. And he'd remind him, without having to even think or say it — though of course he believed it to be true — of what a failure he was for still living with him at thirty. He'd badger him about never getting around to earning his teaching certificate like he'd insisted he do as soon as he finished his degree, which was why he just sat around twiddling his thumbs all day. And he thought it's bullshit, it's all such bullshit.

His father would be back by midday. Jan thought that maybe it'd be better for him not to stick around. It'd seem like he hadn't done anything productive. He got in the shower and let water stream down his body, though it did little for his zits or the bags under his eyes. He dressed in a hurry and headed out without copies of his résumé in hand. He didn't know where exactly he was going, only that he felt somewhat propelled by a verse from the book that had kept him up the night before: "Paths and trails call me to the toilsome wandering, asking…"

There was the buzz of carrer Francesc Macià. The opening and closing of storefronts. People walking up and down, towing their shopping carts behind them. And cars not finding a place to park along the narrow road beneath the belltower. But he didn't want to see anyone. He walked up carrer de Dalt, towards the mountain. He knew the old buildings would be empty. The streets would be quiet there, wide and comfortable, solitary and lost.

An old lady fed the cats on the grounds of the boarded-up Cal Blai manor. And up ahead, on an abandoned patio, the mallow was in bloom. Then there was an irrigation canal, now dry and dusty, that would forever remain quiet.

"Off to see your sister, eh?" the old lady pried while letting the catnip she had pooled in her apron fall onto a large, dirty plate on the ground.

"Have you seen her, ma'am?" he asked, suddenly interested as he wondered at the parade of black, grey and white cats beginning to poke out from behind the plants and walls.

"Lord knows that woman spends all day out in the field like an animal. We neighbours can't even catch a glimpse of her," the lady said, a smirk framed by locks of unruly, white hair.

"Have a nice day!" He fled up the street while the old lady turned a little potful of fish bones onto the plate, feeding all those cats that belonged to no one.

"Goodbye, *nen*, goodbye…"

He kept walking, unsure of where he was headed, until he reached the end of carrer de Dalt. The car wasn't parked outside Anaïs's house, and he didn't detect any movement through the window beside the desk in the study. Was she out in the vineyard again? And what about Foix? Would Anaïs remember to pick her up from school at lunchtime? He kept walking toward the outskirts of town. The sheep had left black pellets on the asphalt. He could dodge them, but nothing would save him from the stench of chicken coops. Out in the distance, the town of Sant Jaume looked puny atop a sea of leafless vineyards. Some had already been trimmed. Others were just branches with no leaves, pointing in every direction like stars.

With every step he took, his disbelief grew. There was no way. It couldn't all just vanish. And not under concrete, at the very least. What would happen to the plane trees and the grass beside the rushing stream? How would they look next to all that grey? Where would the goats and hens go? And the pigs and chickens? Where would the mills, the wire fences and shoddy old hoses end up? What good was the water in the wells now that it wouldn't go to filling the reservoirs? Where would the yammering dog guarding the sheep live? What fresh produce would they eat if not pomegranates, apricots, almonds and grapes?

From Quatrecases, he peered out at the Twin Mountains, quelled under the soft midday sun. A slope separated the two mountains, pulling them apart, exposing the pale rocks in the fleeting, January light. Llobeta Vineyard was right up ahead. Maybe he'd see Anaïs there again, looking for bits and pieces of pottery. Or who really knew what she was looking for there? He couldn't get that look of hers out of his head — the suspicion in her eyes when they asked her what she was doing there, and her insistence that those shards held historic value. As if her life itself were at stake. She wouldn't let go. When they'd kept on asking, her silence could have sliced through the air like a knife. As if to her, none of them was even there. She was fixated on the land and her secret discovery. She had to keep watch lest someone steal it from her... As if people were lining up to get their hands on that dusty old rubble, as their father called it — bits of clay polished by the rain.

He couldn't yet make out Llobeta Vineyard when he heard the cries. It was a woman's voice, and she seemed irritated. It seemed like she was talking to someone, but he could only make out *her* voice. And the closer he drew, the more it sounded like Anaïs. He picked up the pace, no longer trying to avoid the black pellets on the ground.

The stone partitions, bare from winter, provided a good view. Anaïs kept yelling and yelling, her voice harmless and fierce at the same time. He saw her from behind, looking out at the forest that climbed up the Twin Mountains and twisted through the Marmellar Valley, the Castellot Range, and the roads to the Santa Maria de Foix church. She kept yelling, "Get out, Miquel, and don't come back!"

"Anaïs, who are you talking to?"

"Look, he's walking between the trees!"

"I can't see anyone. Who is it?"

"Over there, over there!"

Jan kept walking towards where she'd said, but he didn't see anyone. He went into the forest and picked up his pace until he broke into a run, shoving aside the branches, skirting rocks, hopping over puddles. Then he heard a noise, unsure if it belonged to a person, a squirrel or a wild hog.

He turned towards the noise and the mountain fell quiet. "All omen, here, the forest's voice, with the leafless dialect of roots, it speaks darkly, the arcane." The poetry from his book came to him again — there, in the middle of it all.

Anaïs spoke of a Miquel, but Jan never saw him. He wanted to find out who the hell he was, but he was tired of running. He came to a stop in the middle of that overgrown path, squatting with his hands on his knees, his breath quick. If he *was* real, he'd escaped him that day. She kept saying that he'd come from the farms, from the mountains or from Pi de Llobets, and that he'd always shuffle back the way he came. That he strolled the vineyards and sometimes talked to Foix and pretended he was Grandpa Pau. And that he wanted to rob the shed. That she'd even caught him inside there, poking around her "valuable" collection of ancient, shattered pottery on a few occasions. It was as if he were a ghost. But she insisted that she'd kept running into him and that they'd talk and he'd try to act nice, but she didn't trust him one bit because he was out to steal from her. Separating from her husband must have affected her. Because no, that was not the sister he knew. She'd become obsessed with saving the vineyard from the Logistics Centre, and nothing could stop her. She spent more time out at the vineyard than at home. People in town were talking. She was digging for odd little pebbles… and now she had imaginary friends, to boot!

He looked up. Sweat streamed down his forehead. A couple of birds chirped on the highest branches. The puddles reflected a quiet that refused to leave. Anaïs had seen Miquel. And Miquel wasn't there. The forest was dark and the road was empty. Anaïs was losing it.

If Samira were there, they could have gone out to the lookout point or to the beach, where he would have told her everything.

She returned to her office. The fluorescent yellow of the highlighter, visible only halfway into the court ruling, compelled her to finish her remaining tasks. But she preferred to open her email. Jordi's call had piqued her curiosity. The young hire had been quite thorough. He'd written down the entire case while she'd been smoking at the bar in a tucked-away square downtown. Maybe their professional relationship had started with a hierarchical air, but she didn't feel bad about it. He would have to learn by doing, undoing and messing up — although many hated Elisa for being so high-handed.

There was an "A." in the subject line, and she thought that poor Jordi's superiors must have only taught him the bare minimum about the norms of confidentiality. When she saw how the message unfurled on the screen like a bible, she realised he'd gone overboard. She furrowed her brow, glanced at the pigeons on the balcony, then found herself feeling a bit disconcerted by the noise on the other side of the door, of the overbearing people bothering the secretary whose frenzied, stressed countenance was now the face of the institution. She thought that everyone must be going crazy.

At first, having to read the whole email seemed unnecessary. Time was worth more than gold when each of her days was brimming with cases of systemic poverty and violence, all set against the general turmoil of the news. Information was constantly overflowing all around her, from her hefty coat, her tiny desk, her run-down office and from the town of El Vendrell itself. Court rulings, the far right, email, abuse, case reports, painful memories, the national road, rejected pigeons, climate change, the heartbreak and disillusion that crept up further every day. But she softened her gaze as soon as she began reading because, in the end, *she* had to put up with everything.

The doctor's patient was called Anaïs and she was forty years old. It was her father, Senyor Magí, who'd set up the appointment, not her. He wanted to see if there was anything that could be done if she refused help. Jordi's writing was conversational, and he had yet to polish his administrative voice, the amateur. He was clearly breaking professional norms, but since the story had caught her attention, she spared him the snotty response he deserved.

He wrote that the woman's behaviour was far from normal. *And what does "normal" mean, kid?* She said things that didn't make much sense. *Did they teach you the meaning of "sense" in college, you little brat?* She was constantly in distress, irritated by everything around her and mad at the world for the impending loss of her family's vineyard. *Another wannabe psychologist, damn it!* Everyone saw it differently: according to Anaïs, she was acting like that because of the Logistics Centre, but according to her father, it was due to a recent marital separation. *Father and daughter in disagreement, it's the end of the world as we know it!* Their breakup had been sudden and for no good reason. *Oh, what a huge problem, and how uncommon, too, young man...* The patient was obsessing about losing the vineyard and had started acting very strangely, collecting pieces of old pottery, but who knew what they even were, really? *How lovely!* She'd scream at strangers trespassing the vineyard grounds. *What a warrior!* And she'd imagined some of those strangers. *Ooooh, ghosts?* She'd spend hours working the land with obsessive attention and care, respecting all of her deceased grandfather's practices. *Holy moly!* And her seven-year-old daughter, Foix, was suffering the consequences. She was often left on her own at home and had to ask other relatives for help. *A resourceful girl, however.* And Anaïs would get aggressive when anyone questioned her attitude. *Oh really, an aggressive woman, how strange, right?*

After skimming the email, she found herself cursing that young specialist who'd flouted confidentiality protocol and hastily proposed an intervention, all while demonstrating his inexperience, ineptitude, incompetence and lack of professionalism, on top of his general male chauvinism and presumptuousness. It seemed more like a journal entry than a work email. She spit malicious words at the ceiling so she wouldn't have to ask what the hell was wrong with separating, like she had, and what the hell was wrong with loving the land instead of someone who didn't love you back.

A woman who was separated, like her. A woman who was separated, who possessed some obsessive habits that seemed, to most people, the result of being alone. Alone like her. She couldn't find the patience to start typing up a response, or to go back to underlining the court ruling from the other case. She got up from her chair, left her office, crossed the waiting room with a less arrogant air than earlier that morning — or any other day — and went down the stairs. No one, neither the secretary nor the overbearing folks at reception, said a thing to her. They would've been in for a rough ride if they had. She was in the break room with the microwave and a mug of water and a teabag. And she felt pleased as she looked at the pigeons on the balcony. Those diseased birds surrounded the entire building to remind her that Mateu had left her, like a person shooing away the birds at a terrace bar. She didn't even hear the ding of the microwave. Anaïs's story had crept into her like the chill of that grey winter morning.

He tapped open his conversation with Samira.

Winter had passed. Now she was rarely online, but he'd been lucky that day. Though the cold months were behind them, Jan let March weigh down on him all the same. Anaïs was losing it. Samira was growing distant. He thought of his mother, turning the idea of her over in his head. She'd died in childbirth so he might live. Before, though, what had her relationship with Anaïs been like? Was he supposed to feel guilty? He couldn't bring himself to. He'd never known her enough to miss her. And it wasn't his fault he'd been born. Did that make him cold blooded? A monster, even?

But that wasn't what really mattered now. He had to know what it'd been like for Anaïs. How could one measure the exact experience of loss? He had to know if Anaïs had got past it. He needed a way to understand her strange behaviour. Maybe she had never reached full emotional maturity. Or she was emotionally stunted, in any case. And that was why she'd divorced Foix's father. Of course. Maybe she was immune to loss, because nothing would ever be as devastating as losing her own mother. And since nothing would ever be that tragic again, she could toss out a man like any old sock. Yes, that was it. Perhaps she needed something to hold onto. The vineyard, the shed, the threats looming over the countryside. Of course. She'd already been orphaned by her mother and she wouldn't be orphaned by the land as well.

Samira: Stop with your bullshit! You should read over your texts before you hit send!

Jan: What's wrong? What did I say?

Samira: Anaïs told you how sexist it was that you asked why she would ever leave a man who had "never abused her." And you can't take it. You're trying to psychologise her!

Jan: And what else am I supposed to do?

Samira: Get out more. Don't waste your time (I'm not wasting mine). If you're worried about Anaïs, you should at least attempt to set your own hang-ups aside.

Jan: And how do I do that?

Samira: You could start by paying attention to the land.

Jan: Paying attention to the land? You're crazy…

Samira wasn't getting it. It was March and Anaïs was worse than she'd been in December. Samira had left before then and couldn't understand — her anthropology fellowship involved a different skill set. She'd moved away. What gave her the right to preach at him like that, when he was the one who had to put up with all this crap? Then, out of nowhere, he calmed down. He gazed at the screen. It wasn't right to dismiss her just because she wasn't there. She was always at least partially right… but he grew uneasy again. And to top it off she'd said she wasn't wasting time. What did that mean? Had she gone out with other guys? As if he hadn't figured as much already! If they weren't even a couple, why should he care?

His father came home.

"Hello, son. Send out a lot of résumés today?"

"Jesus!" Jan slammed his laptop shut and got up from the couch. "Why am I still living with you? I'm thirty, dammit!"

He grabbed a beach bag and started rummaging all over the house, grabbing things and stashing them inside. And before he walked out the door, he remembered — the anthology. He went up to his room and chucked the book in his bag before storming out and getting in the car, calling the verses to mind: "Once again I'm at the place I always come to when I slowly descend to the small cellar in the house of my mind."

The bag sagged on the seat. The roundabouts on the national road were unforgiving. He thought about his relationship with Samira, which always came and went. In the bottleneck traffic between the two largest ports in the country, Jan fantasised about being tragically squashed to death under a truck. What else could happen in this free-for-all? Their relationship always came and went and now there was nothing to show for it, he thought. Factories and warehouses marred the pine groves. The grapevines had all shrivelled up from the drought. He could sense a layer of smog covering the entire region. He focused on the white line painted on the asphalt. She was gone, and she wrote less by the day. He clung to the steering wheel. She'd said that she needed to see the world, that her parents had smothered her for years... And on the left-hand side, he saw a sex worker's shadow on the curb. He tried to avoid eye contact.

He passed the final roundabout on the national road and the last crossroads of that seaside neighbourhood, then he parked by the still uninhabited beach at the marsh near Les Madrigueres. The estuary that'd been swallowed up by the drought propped up a concrete wall covered in graffiti. There'd been plenty of progress with the efforts to restore the wetlands and dunes since he'd last been there. The white houses, bidding farewell to their season of quiet, had their blinds down to block out the summer dwellers, their empty terracotta pots on the balconies. A sea cormorant scavenged for food among the reeds in the marsh, while a Kentish plover soared over the dunes and brush, seeking out the hidden lagoon. And Jan found refuge in the only untouched mile of that mangled coast, like an Audouin gull in the scrubland.

Endangered birds nested, migrated and returned there. He remembered Samira lying between the sea and the marsh, right where the fresh and saltwater meet. She'd migrated and he could forget about building a future with her. The endangered birds raised their hatchlings there, just like his parents had raised Anaïs, and then they'd leave, like his mother. He had survived like an endangered species. And he thought that sometimes families fall apart. And that everything comes and goes and that cement threatened to smother the region where he'd always lived. And that his wings were being cut — by the employment crisis, by love, by all the chaos in his family life.

He walked across the sand and laid out a beach blanket right near the water. There was nobody but him. A few boats had been left upside down, beached like dead whales. From far away, another group of stationary boats gathered their masts, pointing toward the sky like arrows from a bygone war. Just a few devoted fishermen and the waiter from Can 60, wiping tables apathetically, remained. He imagined that their routines weighed on them like the clouds over the marsh in winter, robbed of the dunes by tourism. He looked at the horizon. Why the fuck was the ocean blue? Why couldn't it be another colour, one that wouldn't swallow him up?

The peak of Montmell stood far in the distance. He could see it. One day Samira had pointed it out as she swam in the waters stilled by winter. "Look, Jan, Montmell is right in front of me, straight ahead!" she'd said, water dripping from her fingertips as she used one arm to balance herself in the soft waves. The opaque water hid the boulders that once stood on the river's bygone expanse of sand. The boulders were annoying. And they climbed on each other's backs, like little kids, so as not to hurt their feet. Then they'd lain on the sand, the sea lapping at their feet — the sea their excuse. As well as that simple walk and the protected area and the birds from the marsh. Samira had abandoned her hair to the breeze like the tufts of marram grass, and her round breasts had flattened in the sun, like the dunes. A thread of sand, thin and straight, had fallen from his fingers onto Samira's outstretched arm, onto the soft skin of someone he'd later forget and then remember to call — every so often, at the precise moment, with the right words, for the perfect amount of time, like an exact caress. And he thought about how everything's ephemeral and cyclical and a pile of shit at the same time. Like the cycle of the kingfisher nesting in Les Madrigueres. Like the threat of extinction looming over the Iberian killifish and Kentish plover and all the other endangered species in this world. Meanwhile the mallard duck didn't migrate; it waited. And it wasn't thirty years old.

THE BONFIRE

He only had a few years left until he retired, but he should have done so right that morning as he walked to the store, weary as he was from living. He dreamt of being able to take care of the vineyard, enjoy time with his granddaughter or simply know that something in his life had made it all worth it. Like having become a widower, with a ten-year-old daughter and newborn to care for. Then having shepherded them both onward, pushing them towards life with all his might. That Magí, what a great father, the town would say. And now what? He'd gone to work each morning in order to bring up his children, Jan and Anaïs. Working the register at the co-op, weighing fresh fruit, scanning barcodes and serving white wine. And red wine, and vermouth and muscatel. All in bulk. All from this very land. You could fill a one- or two-quart bottle. The people were lovely and grateful, and it was a pleasure. What good was it now? His son was lost and his daughter was going nuts.

He'd talked with the other co-op members to see if there was any work for Jan, but a financial crisis was on the horizon and it was better not to bring anyone on. He'd spoken with Anaïs's physician to say, "Doctor, she's not well but she's saying nothing's wrong, what can we do?" Then the doctor had told him, "It doesn't seem all that serious, Magí, it's hard if she doesn't come to the clinic herself, but I'll check with some folks and get back to you." Though he still hadn't called back after two months. And Anaïs kept doing strange things. They'd talk about her in the shop, whisper about her all around town. On that morning in March when he'd wished he'd already retired and was walking to work — his eyes on the ground, his son lost and his daughter going nuts — he couldn't get her off his mind. And when he looked upward — suddenly, his gaze unfocussed — he saw it.

It was far off, but he could sense a fire at the foot of the Twin Mountains. Smoke streamed from Vilarer, blotting out the sky. It looked like it was coming from Llobeta Vineyard. Like there was a brush pile on fire, but he was in town, and he was the only one in the family who had burned the brush in the last twenty years. He felt startled. I'm too old for these kinds of scares, he muttered. He had always been the one to set the bonfire, ever since his father had died. Twenty years of making sure to get rid of the sticks as best he knew how, getting a permit from town hall to burn them there, at the foot of the Twin Mountains. Whoever was doing it was being reckless, and that person surely hadn't got a permit either, which would only mean a big mess for him, the owner.

He took off running. The shop didn't matter. His manager, colleagues, the co-op members and kids there to buy breakfast would have to wait or run along or do without him. It had been three months since Anaïs had got all worked up at Llobeta Vineyard and had convinced him not to accept the buyout. But he couldn't get that look of hers out of his head — her skin flushed in otherworldly anger. He ran and ran towards the fire, imagining Anaïs there, the perpetrator of that unforgivable, careless act. What was happening to his Anaïs? Why did she suddenly care so much about the vineyard after leaving him to take care of it for all those years? She was focusing all her attention on Llobeta Vineyard because in a few months it would be destroyed, but something still escaped him. His daughter was already forty and had always had a good head on her shoulders. How could she possibly think that tending the vineyard now would stop the construction?

Poor thing, she'd lost her mother at ten, and he'd been left to care for a young girl and a baby. Maybe he hadn't done things right and now his children were turning the tables on him. A madwoman and a moocher. What shit luck, for the love of God! And the angrier he felt inside, the faster he ran towards the fire that was already in sight, past the roads and paths and banks and bends. And when he got there, surrounded by that place, he wished things were different. If only the Logistics Centre could be built in a way that respected nature and the people in the region. But he also thought about how the vineyard was unprofitable, so it was all just a dog chasing its own tail, a vicious circle. What would've been the perfect solution? He said *would've* been because he was convinced that in a few months the construction equipment would arrive and everything would collapse under a layer of concrete. That would happen whether he wanted it to or not. And many farmers, like him, had already accepted the loss.

He saw Anaïs at the far end of the vineyard, contemplating the flames that burned through the brush pile and branches. As if that weren't enough, the tractor was parked on the other side. Who had given her permission to take his tractor out? She sure had some nerve. And no one had even shown her how to drive it!

The vines, now cleared, exposed their dark branches, signalling towards the sky like open fists. The blackness drove all colour from the earth. He stood there, baffled before the fire imprinting itself on the cold landscape. Pumpkin-coloured flames and streams of grey smoke blotted out the sky — far too close to the partition, to the open brush and to the carob tree, for his liking. It was nonsense, madness, a nightmare. She was planted there, believing that her presence could control the fire. But no, she, his eldest, hadn't the slightest idea of how to oversee a fire, how to cut the brush and sticks back, how to drive that big ole thing. He ran towards her, screaming all the while. Had she gone mad? But Anaïs didn't even glance his way. And he insisted. He insisted with the kind of fervour that kept him insisting until she answered. And she looked at the fire, and the ground, and the fire and the ground, and she said, "Alright already, you can stop." She'd hitched the tractor to the wheel hoe, which she'd taken from her grandparents' yard, and had driven it up the path, up the road to Quatrecases, all on her own, in the dark of early morning, without a word to anyone. And maybe she'd never done it before but she'd learned from watching others doing it time and time again. She wanted to let the grapevines breathe again, passing the wheel hoe through the field row by row, carefully turning around at the turnrow, slowly but surely. Then he cut her off. He wouldn't let her get another word in. And not because he was angry, not because he was a man, not even because he was her father. He cut her off in a panic because the fire was growing far too big, and it was spreading towards the partition, spreading into the open brush, the brush bursting into flames and edging toward the carob tree. And as both of them ran off to find shovels in the hut, he told her that she'd gone too far this time. You should've let me know, an open fire like this should be on flat land and surrounded by dirt and rocks. She grabbed two shovels and gave him one without even glancing his way. They dug up dirt and threw it on the fire near the partition and on the bonfire pit too, lest it grow wild once more.

He turned on the TV, lighting up his pale, olive skin as Foix played on the couch.

It was April and the unemployment rate in the region had skyrocketed to the highest in the country. Some people said the Logistics Centre would bring more work, but Jan knew that the warehouses would end up locked and empty. Every word spoken inside would merely echo in the hollow of that lifeless field they'd built, where someone, at some point, would eventually realise that money can't be eaten. But at the platform's meetings, which at least kept his mind busy, he could tell that people were starting to give in. The land had already been compulsorily purchased. It wouldn't be long before the bulldozers arrived.

Anaïs was also worrying him. But why? What was the point of this nightmare? Anaïs's doctor had finally put their father in his place, saying that it wasn't such a big deal, that nobody would lift a finger for her case. If the problem persisted and got worse, they could call again. But Jan couldn't get his sister's obsession out of his head. At first, he thought his father had overstepped. But then he reconsidered. If she couldn't recognise the problem, maybe they *did* have to do something about it.

The news on the TV filled him with rage. Foix was playing with her teddy bear. She couldn't understand what they were saying on the television, and the teddy bear bored her because it couldn't talk, walk or pee, and she couldn't go looking for fun because lunch was almost ready. She didn't have any toys around. It was just him and his dad living there. Poor little Foix. Fuck this life and the brainwashing on the news. He didn't feel like reading either. He picked up his laptop and looked over the contacts in his chat box. Judit. Judit… She'd been a grade behind him in school. They'd never talked about all that nonsense. She lived in Barcelona and didn't come to Vilarer much. What was she up to in life? Was she hot?

The sofa was big. His entire leg fit on it. And both of Foix's of course. But she was starting to get antsy because her teddy bear was boring her. Jan clicked on the photograph on Judit's profile. She was very good looking. He opened the chat. He thought about saying, Hey, Judit, what are you up to, what's life like, when are you coming to Vilarer? But Foix flung herself on his shoulders and balanced on top of him as if he were a pony. He put his hand on her belly and lifted her into the air. She could almost touch the ceiling, and she laughed and hollered, wriggling her arms around to free herself, which meant *yes, yes, let's play*. He said that he'd toss her out the window. She said that she wanted a pony ride. So Jan got down on his hands and knees and Foix straddled his back. First they went up the hallway, then down. They shrieked and laughed and nobody could hear them and they couldn't hear anyone either, because on the other side of the wall, the kitchen window was letting out the first rush of steam from a rice dish filled with meat and fish and vegetables under the growing rumble of the range hood.

The four wooden sides of the kitchen window framed a radiant day, an impeccable sky, unflinching trees and desert paths. Everything was in its place. April had imposed its luminous and rapidly spreading deep green. Anaïs and her father had poured in the broth, which was now bubbling on the stove, turning the pan into a container of upside-down rain — every grain a larva, the rice a flat mountain.

"You guys don't care about anything," Anaïs declared. And her father replied, "And you do? You spend all day poking around for rubble."

The rice boiled.

She said, "It's not rubble. It's-not-rub-ble," as she sliced a fuet sausage, fluttering the knife up and down. Then pointed her finger at her father while vowing that she'd put a stop to the construction with those ceramic relics. A spoon in hand to test whether the rice was done, her father said the bulldozers were at the ready, and that this wasn't how things should be done, this wasn't the way to stop them. She raised her voice, her tone, her arms and the knife and said that if he wanted to save the land, he had to love it first. Her father replied that she shouldn't have lit the bonfire without him and covered the pan. And she said, "I can't burn grapevines or drive the tractor; what else can't I do?" But her father always had a comeback and retorted that, for starters, she could quit making up intruders, and he wiped his hands dry with a cloth and crossed his arms as he leaned back on the sink. But she wasn't seeing things, no, and she said so as the rice swelled up inside the pan like a rolling field, and the hood muffled Foix's laughter in the background, behind the door where everything seemed normal, though her apron was gross, and the fuet knife moved up and down: "What-the-hell-else-can't-I-do?"

Fuet and olives scurried from the middle of the table as their father began to pile everyone's plates with steaming rice. Foix cared little about conversation, happy just to sit there quietly, giggle, and offer up her plate so that it'd be given back to her piled high with food. Jan was lost in thought. Anaïs wondered what whirlwinds of emotion were muddling his head. Her father fell silent and ate. He seemed happy enough that everyone was there, gathered around the table. Anaïs thought this was the right time to explain what was eating her up inside.

She'd had enough with that conversation in the kitchen, but this matter was such a huge, monumental deal that everyone would certainly offer to help her right away and fix it all up. She was worried about the rabbit plague that had been threatening the grapevines for days now. Though her father said that she was exaggerating, that there'd always been wild rabbits in Penedès. How could she even entertain the notion that a vineyard as old as theirs would be endangered by a couple of rabbits, poor little creatures, what a thing to say. But she insisted that the rabbits would eat the shoots, those that April was just drawing out, and that it wasn't unheard of in vineyards with vase-form pruning, and that her grandfather always said that it could be catastrophic if it wasn't stopped. And then it wouldn't be the Logistics Centre's bulldozers destroying the grapevines, but the rabbits, because without shoots there'd be no grapes, then there'd be no point in taking care of them, defending them or saving them at all. But her father said he'd never witnessed any rabbits ruining the harvest for an entire year. Never. Anaïs insisted that it was possible, because her grandfather had always said that it could happen. So he said that he was sorry, that he didn't know of any tricks for such an occasion, meaning, forget it, sweetheart.

She could fix it with dog poop. She remembered her grandfather. She remembered him telling her that. She could ward them off with dog poop, soaked and spread out on the grapevines using an old broom. At night. It had to be done by night. Yes, rabbits were repelled by the stench of rehydrated dog poop. She swore it to them. It was a fine repellent. They would see. Foix stuck out her tongue and said, "That's gross." Jan and her father's teeth ground to halt. They'd stopped chewing on the rice, their mouths shut, lips round, eyes agog, as if she were growing stranger by the day. They told her she was making that up, that she shouldn't be telling tall tales. But Grandpa Pau had told her that once, twenty years ago. She could remember. So they told her she was losing it. But she said she was going to test out the old trick, whether they liked it or not.

FOIX

He ran towards Anaïs's house in the hopes of finding her there, as he hadn't heard from her in weeks.

April had come and gone and she hadn't picked up any calls. Luckily, he had a spare key. The entire first floor stank of animal faeces. That the house had been a pigsty for those last few months was an unpleasant fact, sure, but he had handled it better than this. He walked through the entryway, looked in the storage room, scanned the backyard...nothing at all. When he opened the garage door, the smell's source became clear. Some twenty plastic bags bursting with poop. It didn't make any sense. Wasn't it enough for his sister to collect broken pieces of pottery from a long-gone past? Why did she have to go and gather bags of shit, too? Maybe all that talk about old tricks to get rid of rabbits wasn't a joke after all. Was he dreaming? Was she crazy? Was he crazy? Her modern house didn't fit that image, that smell. He stared at the piles of bags and, suddenly, he saw a light-brown ponytail with a colourful scrunchie shifting among them. He approached in disbelief. Yes, it was real. A barefoot Foix was playing with Lego in the middle of all that mess, amid the broken pottery pieces, the bagged-up animal shit.

"Anaïs, Anaïs, Anaïs!" he screamed while running up the stairs. No response from the floor above either. And nothing had changed over the last few months. The little pieces of pottery scattered on the dining room floor. Dishes from the past few days stacked on the marble counter in the kitchen. Dirty laundry piling up in Foix's room. And from her school backpack, unzipped, a week's worth of half-eaten sandwiches spilling out.

He went back to the garage and put his hand on the back of Foix's neck. Feeling assured, she didn't say a word. "Let's go, little lady." And they left. He had to take care of Foix and ignore that never-ending nightmare. Maybe he'd have found Anaïs in the vineyard, but he didn't want to go out looking for her because it wouldn't do any good. She'd keep on saying that her historic find would save the vineyard from the compulsory purchase. She'd get angry with him for even doubting her and look at him as if he weren't even there. The breeze from the foot of the mountain would tangle up the hair she no longer took care of. But she'd say that her breakup with Foix's father had nothing to do with it. Then she'd insult him like when they were kids if he brought up going to the psychologist again.

But Foix asked about her mama. Then there was the ignition, the clutch, the shift into first gear. Even though none of it would do any good. There was the pedal, the smoke, the noise. Even if she'd get angry with him for doubting her. There was the street corner by their house, the last corner of the neighbourhood, third gear, fourth and fifth. Even if she insulted him like when they were kids. There were the farms and the immense waves of green swelling towards Sant Jaume, towards Quatrecases, nestled at the foot of the Twin Mountains. Even if she looked at him as if he weren't there. There was Lloveta Vineyard, the key, the gears in neutral, the handbrake.

There was Anaïs. Though Jan couldn't remember how they'd even got there. She told him to leave her alone. "And what's going on with Foix?" he asked. "Well take her with you then," Anaïs replied. That there was no need to worry. She'd come and get her before dinner. On her word.

Foix grabbed her teddy bear and hugged it tightly. The landscape flashed past them like a movie. Sheep were blocking the road and the shepherd ushered them to one side for the car to pass, his crook in the air and his loyal dogs by his side. The sky suddenly cloaked everything in darkness — the road to Quatrecases, the Twin Mountains, the power lines grazing the sky, the cyclists and the runners on their way back to town.

They took off with the moon on their tail, the sheep returning home with their heads bowed. Perhaps the sheep, unlike the cyclists and the runners, would have wanted to take in the luminous moonlight. Sheep flocked together, while Foix's mother was all alone. The swallows had flown back from the south and passed over Quatrecases, their trills sounding out again beneath the old balconies. Like Great-Grandpa Pau and the birds from Les Madrigueres and Uncle Jan's friend. And Uncle Jan was taking her to her grandfather's house, where she'd have a good time for sure. They'd told her that her uncle lived with her grandfather because he was a moocher. Maybe being a moocher meant being a little kid. If that was the case, she also wanted to be a moocher, so she could always be little, and live with her mother forever.

It was also getting dark in town. She was lucky to be going over to her grandfather's house, where she could sit on the couch with her teddy bear, watch cartoons before dinner and play with her uncle. The blinds were already lowered — no one wanted to leave their house. A few bars were still open, Uncle Jan said that they'd be open for longer when the weather was better, but she had school tomorrow, and he'd play with her, then her mother would come over to eat dinner with her and tell her a story before bed. She thought about how lucky she was, how giddy, how happy she felt as Jan unbuckled her seatbelt and took her into the house with him.

Grandpa Magí was grumbling to himself amid the din of pots and cooking utensils. He asked Jan what Anaïs had been up to all evening long, and what could be so important that she had to leave Foix. But Foix knew that her mother would come to get her and that her grandfather was angry because he was bitter. Yeah, he was bitter, which meant getting into other people's business so he didn't have to deal with his own. That's what her mother had told her, her mama, who was the best person in the world after her papa, because her papa had so much work to do and so little time to see her but the first thing he'd do whenever he was done was be with her. That's what her mama had told her. And she was convinced that her mama was so, so, so good, and that she was always right.

Jan was typing on his computer. She thought that if he was really a moocher, then he must like cartoons. How could he be so focussed if there were cartoons on TV? He said he was writing to Samira, and Foix thought that maybe they were boyfriend and girlfriend. But that maybe moochers couldn't be boyfriends or girlfriends because they had to live with their parents. She'd made up her mind: she'd be a moocher. And she hung her arms around his neck, like a ring, and he put his phone on the coffee table so it wouldn't fall to the floor as he tried to keep his balance. And they both spread their arms out and pretended they were aeroplanes, then boats and spaceships, then warriors, horses and riders.

It was dinner time. There was soup, an egg-and-potato truita and salad. Also three plates, three forks, three spoons, three glasses and a pitcher. Her belly was growling. They were still waiting on her mother, but she probably would have already eaten dinner, late as it was. She was so lucky, so incredibly lucky, to have been able to eat her egg-and-potato truita there, at night, with her teddy on the table. She looked at the little hand of the clock, which moved one space past nine. Her mama would get there soon and take her home to put her to bed. But their calls went unanswered, both from her uncle's mobile and her grandpa's and from the landline of that house where Foix could sit calmly and eat her soup, egg-and-potato truita and salad. That house where she was no longer all that calm because her mama hadn't arrived. And it was beginning to upset her. Her mama couldn't abandon her, she just couldn't, that wasn't allowed! She'd come get her and there wasn't any other option in the whole world. And Jan ate quickly and went out looking for her so that Foix would calm down. But there was no answer, not at home or on her phone or from over the hedge of their garden. When Grandpa Magí told her that her uncle hadn't had any luck finding her, she started to cry and grabbed her teddy and went down the stairs. And her grandfather followed behind her and told her not to make a scene in the middle of the street when it was so late, as the neighbours would hear her. And Foix said she wanted her mama, mama, mama and nothing but her mama. Grandpa Magí covered his face with his hands and turned back toward the door. He said that he couldn't take her to her mother because he didn't know where she was. So Foix sat down in the middle of the street, wrapped her arms around her legs and cried. Every so often, she'd peep through her legs to see if her grandfather had walked back towards her, was standing at the door or had gone inside. But he was still at the door. And then she cried even harder. She wanted her mama, mama, mama and no one but her mama. Because she loved her more than anything else on the face of the earth. And in the darkness of her huddled knees, her head between her thighs, she felt a pair of arms picking her up, arms that didn't belong to her mother. Her grandfather's shoulder was comfortable and she was so, so tired. So tired that she didn't even make sure to have her teddy there next to her when she curled up under the sheets.

JUDIT

He walked up carrer de Dalt.

He'd put on a jacket, grabbed the keys, and left Foix with
her grandfather after dinner. He'd rung the doorbell at Anaïs's
house, but no light shone through the windows. He'd screamed
her name — Anaïs! Anaïs! Anaïs! — from the gate. But his cries
failed to conjure up her silhouette in the garden. So he started
down the street, and on his way back, he saw a light on at Fanal
Bar.

He felt like poking his head in, even though he was practi-
cally certain that he wouldn't find any friends there. It was just
another day, a shit day as usual, and most of his friends had
moved abroad or had children, but you never knew. He flung
the door open, not expecting such a surprise. Who would have
thought it? It was her. She was on her way out, a near-empty
beer bottle in hand. It was possible that he hadn't seen Judit since
she'd moved to Barcelona, and he wasn't sure why she'd be in
Vilarer on a normal day like today.

"To what do we owe the honour?" he asked, aware that he
was turning their reunion into small talk.

"Barcelona makes me lonely," she said, leaning on the outside wall and making a puppy face.

The waiter allowed them one last drink as he wiped down the
tables and put the chairs up. Judit was guzzling a beer and rolling
a cigarette while he sipped from his glass of Baileys. Her words
were sparse, as if he wasn't really the right person to tell her life
story to. But they were in Vilarer, facing each other, savouring
the bar's last round. As if she were materialising this thought,
she let herself go, swigging on the beer between phrases. All
words were welcome, and they deserved to tell each other about
their lives in the most banal of ways. She said that everyone

experienced vertigo as they crossed that definitive — and late — bridge into adulthood. Everyone felt lonely; everyone was scared of such times. And he felt the same. He took a gulp of Baileys, ice clinking in his glass. Then he licked his wet lips with a discrete tongue. He spoke of loneliness, aware that the term could encompass anything, allowing him to keep from digging deeper while not quite lying either.

"It's everywhere, Judit."

"What is?"

"Loneliness."

"It is, isn't it?"

"Just look at me."

"But you've got family…" she said, attempting to console him.

"It's a nightmare," he said obscurely.

"Anaïs, huh?" Judith concluded, letting the vox populi pass her lips.

"Rumours from town?" he asked, imagining the old lady on carrer de Dalt gossiping away as she fed those cats that belonged to no one, his aunts and uncles carping on about Anaïs, the clients at the store mumbling under their breath. He pictured them one by one, like sheep crossing the road.

"Don't be mad," she said, trying to soften the mood.

"I don't want the Logistics Centre here either," he proclaimed.

"How come?" she asked, perplexed.

"It'll be devastating, Judit."

"But it'll bring work," she assured.

"There's no way," he went on, firmly.

"Why?"

"Don't you realise? There are other half-empty warehouses in the region…" he insisted, bringing his glassful of ice toward his chest as he leaned in to convince her.

"But this one's promising! There's a wonderful project

behind it," she declared, sure of herself.

"And the little work it will bring will be precarious…" he went on.

"That depends on how you look at it," Judit wavered.

"…and logistics are unsustainable," he concluded.

"But this is the economic model we've got, Jan."

"Maybe it's time we change models."

"Well, you can keep dreaming in the meantime, but you have to take care of Anaïs…"

"What did you hear?"

"They say she's crazy."

He called a few of Vinyoli's verses to mind: "Let us drink from the cup of dreams and die with our final sip." He couldn't tell if he was tired or wanted to go outside and smoke, but he asked Judit if she was ready to get going. They handed their empty glasses to the waiter, who really just wanted to see them out the door. And there, on the street, under the bright sign that read "Fanal," Jan realised that April was only warm by day, despite the banal conversation, the rumours, their argument and all the awkwardness that he hadn't desired from that encounter. April was only warm by day; the night was dark, like bedcovers and making out. So dark that it wouldn't matter if he was making a mistake, because fire would always end in ash. Their comfort depended on them alone.

At the moment they'd have to part ways Judit said that she'd fixed up her parents' attic into an apartment for herself so that she could come by more often, now that she was feeling so lonely in Barcelona.

"I'd love to see it."

"Sounds good."

They didn't talk about what else they might do up there. She seemed happy, and he didn't have to worry. Not about the day before, the day after or about the rumours in Vilarer. And the sky was dark.

They'd opened the door and tiptoed up the stairs. Their mouths met, breath hot, and Jan couldn't remember how it'd all unfolded, what they'd said to each other, though maybe they'd said nothing at all. They pressed their skin together and pulled each other close.

The bed was creaking far too much, excessively, and Judit's parents, snoring downstairs, would hear. So they peeled away the covers, got up, and Judit said she was cold as she dragged the mattress down to the floor in a single, impatient movement. They'd thrown the mattress on the floor and they'd done it quickly, so that they could climb back into their den of blankets, with nothing to say in the seconds in between. Kisses fought against words. A mute tongue against a bitten one. Her breasts on his chest, pressing down on his long, pale body.

THE SHED

He took a deep breath.

The sun peeked through the fogged-up window as light took over the shingles, their colours growing more vivid as the moon faded into sky. Jan teetered between dream and wakefulness as daylight plucked his lashes, and he felt himself reflexively looking at his phone in case he'd received some sign of life from Anaïs. No luck. Judit was asleep on his arm. He had it wrapped around her as if she were important to him. He carefully pulled it out from under her and got up, trying not to make any noise, put on his trousers, and then his sweater and his shoes. She was still asleep.

He ran home and found out that his father hadn't heard from Anaïs either. They took the car, dropped Foix off at school and set out to look for Anaïs until they found her. Her blinds were down and they rang the doorbell again and again, despite the silence that met them. They used their spare key to go inside. The smell in the entryway was still unbearable. Closed doors. Pottery scattered all over the first floor. The kitchen covered in grime. Foix's room like a war zone. The bags of faeces were gone, but the smell remained.

They got back into the car without much to say. Jan put the key in the ignition, but before turning it he glanced at his father, who looked just as baffled. Had Anaïs taken the bags out with her early in the morning? Maybe at dawn? Or had she done so the night before? Their questions clouded around them. Without a word, they agreed that their next stop would be Llobeta Vineyard. And they set off up the road to Quatrecases, though they didn't know what they'd find. Spring was inching forward and the green of the vines on either side of the road grew thicker by the day, splashing further out, wide and almost endlessly, toward Sant Jaume.

The tractor was parked, with some of the foul bags in tow. Not a soul around. The Twin Mountains towered in full splendour on that radiant day, along with every path, slope, rock and tree. The sheep chewed cud on neighbouring farmland, even though it wasn't yet time to graze. April rushed to shake off the cold. The furrows were perfect, bringing order to the sense of wild; the shed remained there, intact, like a stamp of the ages.

His father already seemed to know what they'd find there, but Jan hoped nothing was out of the ordinary, if only so they could go on believing that things were normal, that everyone would go back to business as usual. He walked behind his father between the vines, slowly, with a hand on his shoulder, not wanting to see what he believed he would. They approached the shed, its door ajar, and heard a pattering of stones. The wooden door was cleaner than usual, stripped of dust and dirt, not a single row of ants crawling between the splintered gaps.

The door burst open: "I've got you now, Miquel!"

Anaïs's face relaxed when she saw them.

Jan didn't recognise that look of hers. Anaïs had taught him everything he knew, but she was no longer who she had been — green eyes, serene gaze, fair skin and silky, windblown hair. The one who had founded a design studio so early in her life. Now she was working away in an abandoned shed, her eyes distrustful, clouded over, with frizzy hair to match her jumbled words. She now designed imaginary people, and she still worked meticulously, though her focus was on the pottery.

Seeing that it wasn't Miquel coming towards her, Anaïs sat back down on the ground. Jan couldn't shake his bewilderment. Did this mystery man really exist? Would they see him, in that case? She was sorting the pieces of pottery spread out on the ground before her, sitting on a piece of dirt that felt tidier than before but was still just a den for old, neglected tools. Why had she cleaned it up? Jan didn't understand any of it. Their father looked on in silence, as if pretending to take it all in before expressing the shock that the scene evidently called for. There were no longer spiderwebs on the wall's white, round stones. No bugs, either. No dirt. The old, ramshackle furniture was squeaky clean, with jars of soap and hardwood cleaning spray nicely stored above. What did it all mean? He'd never seen the shed so clean! There had never been cleaning products in there! And canned goods lined the old, ramshackle cabinets. Beans, tuna, olives. Then they pulled the door open wide. The surrealism of the moment sunk in. All the old tools were piled up tightly in a corner, leaving just enough room for a bed on the other side. And that was the oddest thing of all. There had never been a bed there. The shed was no place to sleep.

"Dark brown, over here, pumpkin-coloured, over here, this one has a handle," murmured Anaïs, sitting on the floor and sorting the pieces of pottery while they studied the shed's new arrangement.

"Are you just going to go on sorting without an explanation?" their father asked.

"These two go together... I almost have a complete amphora..."

"Answer us, please. Why'd you bring a bed out here?" Jan asked.

"Light brown, over here, reddish, over here. This is a pitcher spout..."

"Tell us what you're up to all day, damn it!" their father spat, shaking her arms until she responded.

She'd slept there. She'd got there at night. All by herself, winding up the paths. With the tractor and trailer and the old poop trick. By the half-light of the moon above the darkened mountain crest, the shadow of the carob trees and the vernal green of newly-budded plants. She'd sensed a wild boar jumping over the partition but pressed on, fearlessly. She'd smeared all the vines with dog faeces, because she had to fend off the rabbits that would've eaten the new buds and brought about their family's total ruin.

Then Jan realised they needed to stop getting caught up in the matter and asked her why she'd slept in the shed. She said that she wanted to guard the vineyard. In case the construction equipment was brought in to begin work on the warehouse. In case some stranger arrived to rob something from them, from the shed, from the place that belonged to them alone, she added.

"Let's go home, honey. We'll call a therapist," her father said.

"No, I'm staying here until nothing and no one threatens our land."

"And what about Foix?"

"Look after her for a while, will you?"

"You've lost it!" her father said.

"Anaïs… What…what are you even saying, Anaïs?" Jan pleaded.

"And what about Foix's father? What'll he have to say about all of this?"

"Nothing. He lives too far away and her school's here. And it'll only be for a while. She'll be fine with you."

"Jesus Christ…"

"If they want to destroy the shed, they'll have to do it with me inside."

THE ESPRESSO POT

They told the doctor everything.

Jan was beginning to think that his father was right — their last brush-up at the vineyard had marked a point of no return. The Logistics Centre, the land and the struggle were one thing. But his older sister, her health, everything going on in her head... Foix's childhood and everything going on in *her* head, plus everything people were saying in Vilarer, and their reputation — Anaïs's and the family's as well — all that was quite another. Family first, that's right. There was a natural order to things: family before all else.

Anaïs had said she wasn't planning on going to therapy. And that she'd live out in the shed. So he and his father had been forced to take action. They asked all the doctors to come and see it for themselves. With their own eyes, yes. To question Foix until she spit it all out, regardless of whether such treason would make her retch — not just spit. They asked all the doctors to go into the shed, take pictures, jot everything down and do whatever they thought best. And said that if they needed to draft a report, then they should go ahead and make it clear and concise, with all the seals and signatures they saw fit.

May arrived and the fields were succumbing to its verdant insistence. All was lush and leafy, and Jan wore looser clothing. It was supposedly time for him to strike up his springtime activities and start making plans for the summer, but taking care of family matters made him feel useful. He had no money, and Samira was far away.

He watched them arrive at the crossroads by the Country Visitors' Homestead, right where all the roads to each farmhouse met. The dogs started barking on account of their coming — perhaps they'd become used to the quiet, or maybe they'd noticed that the place was abandoned. As they came into view, Jan felt his own doubts inevitably rising. He wasn't confident about what he was about to do. Meanwhile, his father had crossed his tense arms as he watched the medical team walk up the winding road, coming in and out of view through the scrub along the unkempt partitions. His father wouldn't allow a single minute more to pass without solving the problem. He wouldn't allow those people to miss the smallest detail of the spectacle that they were about to witness.

Jan looked at them. He didn't recognise them all. He knew Anaïs's doctor was the stocky one with glasses and that the social worker would be that young and slim one. There were two other women as well. They had a certain elegance about them and must have been around fifty. One seemed more subdued than the other. She looked like a psychiatrist. The other one wore heels but didn't seem to mind the pebbles along the path. Who was she? The remaining three walked up together, and he could hear their whispers and giggles, their expectant faces before this unusual backdrop to their normal workday. She, on the other hand, looked ahead quietly, taking in the mountain's dry and dusty skirt, and the others' backs. She walked surefootedly, provoking unease and respect all at once.

"You must be Jan, right?" said the woman in heels upon their arrival, slicing through the tension as their gazes crossed in the distance. "I'm Elisa, the lead social worker for the region's Northern Area."

He was surprised that she knew his name. He felt a peculiar tremble in his legs. She seemed quite a bit older than him. He couldn't tell if her tone was sweet or dry, or if her upright body was sensual or imposing. He thought that elegance sometimes wasn't a physical shape, but a frame of mind.

"Could you show us to Anaïs, please?" she asked, looking at

him before she turned to continue up the path.

There was the path to the stone hut and there were Jan's eyes. There was Elisa's mini skirt, the curve of her ass, her shapely hips, the dark, translucent tights clinging to her skin. There were the thighs he could intuit, which seemed appealing. There was Jan, who thought that the curve of her thighs was the least of his concerns, because they'd always seem so, given the way she walked among the xarel·lo grapes, leading the pack, her legs not trembling one bit. There was the Llobeta Vineyard. And her high heels caked in the loose soil, proving to everyone that she wasn't afraid of grit. The white rocks lining the skirt of the Twin Mountains clung to the abyss, refusing to let go. There was Elisa's gait, almost at a swing. There was Jan's gaze.

The cartoons on the television seemed to have Foix fully absorbed but Magí closed the kitchen door anyway, so she couldn't hear. As he set the espresso pot on the burner, he tried to convince Jan of the decision they simply had to make. Anaïs had lost her grip on reality when she yelled at the professionals. There was no turning back. They'd seen it all, heard it all, and jotted everything down in their notebooks... Once again, she'd declared that she wouldn't leave the shed until the Logistics Centre's bulldozers showed up and dared to raze everything to the ground with her inside. Magí's daughter had gone completely mad!

The espresso pot started gurgling, with its dark, dense liquid inevitably shooting through the spout. As Magí prepared two mugs, he said that it was all clear to him now, that the situation was out of control and that they had to take matters into their own hands so long as she remained in that state. The television blared in the background, and Jan brought his hands to his face in hesitation. Foix hollered with rage, mimicking the characters on screen and their superpowers. Jan said that the whole thing was crazy. That if they shut Anaïs up in a psychiatric hospital and tore her away from her daughter, she'd get even worse. The cries from the television and Foix and the espresso pot and Anaïs and Jan were blowing up inside Magí's mind too, since he didn't know if *that* was craziness, or if what was actually crazy was everything going on in the shed. But he insisted, he vowed, he maintained that they could not go on like that. Then Jan said that maybe he was right. Maybe it *was* true that Anaïs wasn't recognising the problem, so someone had to do it for her.

On the burning stove, the espresso pot was at the brink of boiling over.

He and his father took a seat in her claustrophobic office.

Elisa shut the door so the noise from the waiting room wouldn't bother them. She was sure to have many visitors throughout the month of May, given that it was the season for scholarships and summer programs. But she received them unhurriedly. Even with visitors waiting on her outside. Even though it was a strange case. Even though it wasn't a matter of life or death.

Jan waited quite some time before opening his mouth. At first he listened, uncertain and somewhat intimidated. His father sought a quick, clear answer. He wanted to know how to control his daughter. Elisa looked at him sternly, glanced at the balcony window, then responded. It was too soon; they had to be patient. On the day they'd visited the stone hut, things had looked a lot differently to her than they had in the email. The doctors had observed depressive traits, but depression wasn't reason enough to act against Anaïs's will. Her father had said that Anaïs had been seeing things, but neither he nor Jan had any proof. Elisa believed that the situation was temporary and that Anaïs would return home as soon as the vineyard was destroyed. But they needed to make some changes, Elisa said. They couldn't allow her to live in the shed for another day. They couldn't allow her to abandon Foix. Or keep avoiding therapy. The girl needed a responsible mother. There was Foix's father too, but he didn't live nearby and Elisa didn't think it necessary to meet with him. Elisa would continue to study the case. She could try to help Anaïs change her behaviour. They should wait and see how things went.

Jan curiously observed the woman who'd just entered their lives. She spoke with just the right words, brief and to the point. But at the same time she needed to study Anaïs's case carefully.

She wasn't completely sure about what she'd read, what she'd seen, what they'd told her about Anaïs, about Foix, about her colleagues' diagnoses. A woman as composed as Elisa had her doubts. But no, Jan was convinced she didn't actually doubt a thing. Maybe she was trying to make it look like she did, just to follow protocol. Maybe she'd been moved by Anaïs's case, or she didn't want to be the bad guy. But no, that was impossible. And if ever she laid the silence bare by looking him in the eyes while she typed, diverting her attention from the screen, he must have been imagining it. It was impossible that she'd notice him for any reason other than Anaïs's case. While he was thinking all of it over, his mother came to mind. The mother who'd be just a bit older than Elisa if she were still alive. The places his mind went, the sheer insanity of it. The years she must have had on him. The child he must have seemed to her.

Minutes passed. The others were growing impatient in the waiting room. Elisa was starting her investigation. She was calmly asking questions, her back to the door. She ignored the complaints coming from the hall, as if they were the whispers of gossiping neighbours. Jan responded, his mouth barely getting the words out. His father spoke with his mouth gaping like a doorless shed letting in the cold. Elisa's protocols poured out of her mouth. And Jan discovered a strange, unfamiliar world. She would send Anaïs a letter with the date and time of her next appointment. If Anaïs didn't show up, she'd follow up three more times. Anaïs would have to sign the letters. It was very, very important. If she didn't show up to the meetings, that would mean she didn't want to be helped. The signed letters would serve as proof if things got out of control, if they ever had to get heavy handed for some reason. Jan asked what would happen after the third failed meeting. What would Elisa end up doing? She'd be compassionate, surely. This woman — averted gaze, beautiful legs, lived-in skin — would do good by Anaïs, no doubt. Jan was looking at her cleavage, unable to take his eyes off it. She looked him in the eyes when she said that if Anaïs didn't show up for the third meeting, she'd go see her at the vineyard.

Jan and Magí had already left the office. She remained there, alone, in front of the notes on her screen. Trying to make sense of it all, to question it. One must always avoid the worst-case scenario, and one must always do what's best for the client, *no matter what*, she thought, propping up her forehead with one hand, a highlighter between her fingers, as she filled out charts in blue pen with the other. Everything depended on her follow-up, which was set to begin right then and there. It was all a matter of whether Anaïs would accept help or not. Anaïs was no longer some separated woman, a victim of stereotypes who was fighting for her land, the way Elisa had viewed her on that winter morning when she first got to know the case. Now she was an obsessive person who'd gone from her design studio in a nice, new house in the country to living in an abandoned stone hut, seemingly overnight. Suddenly, she was spending day and night collecting useless remnants of pottery that she'd found in the nothingness. She was a woman who'd employed unhygienic treatments that came from another sort of nothingness. Who'd imagined intruders and given them names — Miquel, for example. Who'd neglected her house, her daughter and herself. Who'd lost her mother when she was young and who'd just separated from her husband — though all of that, in principle, was just a matter of family history. She wasn't messing around. She was looking for reasons with heft and couldn't give a damn about anything else. The most important reason she'd found was that, following her current obsession, she'd set up house in almost unliveable conditions, in an isolated area with the sole purpose, as Anaïs would say, of stopping the vineyard's destruction at the hands of those building the Logistics Centre. But something was off. All of that should've come straight from *Anaïs's* mouth. A single visit wouldn't do. If she wanted to change Anaïs's life for the better, she'd have to get to know her, talk with her, spend time with her. And if in the end they wanted to put her into treatment against her will, Anaïs would have to show, over the course of a few months, that she didn't want help and that the situation had been going on for a long time, which meant that she'd be wallowing in her own mental breakdown, falling into a bottomless pit. They'd also need a serious diagnosis, which wasn't coming anytime soon, as the doctors thought it was premature. She'd have to be a risk to herself or to others, which meant that they'd all have to turn her in. But that wouldn't happen. She was sure it'd all come to an end when the bulldozers arrived.

She got a notification on her mobile. It was Mateu. "I miss you," he'd written. Rage surged through her. He hadn't said anything like that since he'd left her. What could be going on? "Things didn't pan out with her?" she wrote back. No response, so she kept working.

When she finished up her charts on Anaïs, she lifted her gaze. An image resurfaced in her mind. Who was that boy who'd introduced himself as Anaïs's brother? How old might he be? Thirty? Had he noticed her? Her mind went blank and she stared at the white wall in front of her. She didn't feel like looking at the pigeons, foul and grey as they were. She had the white wall, her slightly drooping eyelids, her lips giving a hint of a smile. No, surely not. She grabbed all the scattered pens at once, closed her fist around them and knocked them against the table to line them up before stashing them in a black, wire jar. She piled up all her papers and filed them away. She adjusted her collar, threw a shawl over her shoulders, and tucked her hair behind her ears. She looked at the pigeons. How dare she let herself feel anything? Who was she kidding?

POTTERY

Jan: How's work going?

Samira: It's great! I'm meeting so many anthropologists from around the world... Summer's just a month away, so my fellowship's ending. I'm planning to travel around Canada, then I might come to Vilarer for a few days in September.

Jan: Oh... And what are your plans for after September?

Samira: I don't know... Life takes so many unexpected turns!

Jan: Right...

Samira: So, what's this big thing you have to tell me? Is Anaïs still living in the shed? Any updates? Oh, and just a heads up, I've got dinner plans, but you said it was something super important, so...?

Jan: Right, about that...remember when we were kids, when we were like ten years old, and we used to play in the shed while the adults were out picking grapes? We discovered some little cardboard boxes with shards of pottery inside, and they were sorted by colour and by where they were found.

Samira: Yes! My secret find! And you didn't seem the least bit interested... Hahaha!

Jan: Earlier that day, you had told me you had a secret to show me. I pestered you about it all day long. And then you finally did. It was almost time to go and Anaïs called us back from the other side of the vineyard, waving her shears in the air. Do you see what I'm getting at?

Samira: Yeah, sounds like her — young, hard-working, intelligent, always smiling. The family's pride and joy. And even way back then, she was already collecting pottery. Don't you think the social worker should know? Shouldn't you be telling *her* this story?

Jan: Right, but do you really think that changes things, considering that she's set up camp in the shed?

Samira: Yeah, I do. Anaïs called us right over. She said it was late and that we had to go. But when we ran back towards the group, they went on picking grapes for a long time. I think what she really wanted was for us to get out of the shed, because it was none of our business.

Jan: Uh-huh…

Samira: You should probably go tell the social worker everything. Tell her that things aren't so clear cut, and that her pottery collection isn't just her latest obsession, or crazy, or dirty, or fake, or useless. I've seen my father do even weirder things at the vineyard! Tell her it's all a matter of perspective.

Jan: Even weirder things? Mohamed?

Samira: One day my father went out at night. My mother got upset because she didn't know where he'd gone. And hours later, he was back. It was the crack of dawn and he smelled like shit, like he'd been in a barn. I've never quite understood it. I still can't quite place the memory.

Jan: Uh-huh…

Samira: And the next day he was cracking up. And my mother got mad at him. And he wouldn't tell her where he'd been. He just kept on laughing like a child. I was drinking a glass of milk at the kitchen table. My mother was in a mood and went out to get groceries. And he looked at me. I asked him where he'd been. He made me swear not to tell my mother. So I agreed. Then he told me he'd spent all night out on the vineyard with your Grandpa Pau. He said they'd smeared dog poop on the grape vines to scare away the rabbits. And then I cracked up, too.

Jan: Shit…

Samira: What?

THE VISIT

The sun's golden light streamed through her office balcony and bathed her uncovered skin and tied up hair, now that the weather was nice. On one side of the table, the letters requesting Anaïs's presence, all signed, were in a pile — the sole proof that she'd refused their support. Elisa would go see her. Because if Anaïs didn't show up to her appointments, Elisa would have to go to her house, as she did with everyone else. The house was a stone hut, but she'd seen worse.

She reviewed every detail of the case, counting on her fingers while staring up at the ceiling. She needed more evidence to back it all up. She couldn't make a fool of herself, she was Elisa — the one who always had her pristine, unbiased notes in order. Nothing got past her, and her signature relayed as much. She had to go there. And as the difficulties of the case, her own demanding standards and every doubt boiled over in her head amid the mess of papers, pens and highlighters, the phone rang. It was the doctor. He said that he and the psychiatrist had gone to see Anaïs. Senyor Magí had called them, worried because construction on the warehouse would start in two weeks, on the 30th of May, and Anaïs was determined to stay put. She wanted to chain herself up inside so the bulldozers couldn't pass, though they didn't know who she had in mind to help her. Maybe someone she'd made up, but who knew, maybe someone from the citizen's platform, someone she trusted, or someone who was just as crazy as she was, or even more so. The doctor said she didn't look well. Unkempt, sad, nervous... she'd lost her way. He'd prescribed antidepressants and given her a referral to a psychiatrist, so he could take his time with the final diagnosis, if there even was one to make.

"Elisa wait, Elisa!" Jan shouted as he crossed the square outside the social work building.

It was first thing in the morning, the stores weren't even open yet, the streets of El Vendrell deserted.

"What are you doing here, Jan? Were you trying to catch me coming into work?" Elisa said with a slightly self-important, flattered smile.

"No, sorry, it's just that I have to tell you something about…" he said nervously.

"About what?"

"Oh nothing, just about the pottery."

"What?"

"So, it, uh, turns out that when Anaïs…well, when Anaïs was doing well…" he stopped.

"Go on…" she demanded.

"Well, nothing, I came to say that Anaïs still isn't planning on coming," he said, relaxing a bit.

"Yes, I know, she's stood me up three times. Is that all?"

On her way to the car, she got a message from Mateu. "I really, really messed up, I was so lost," he'd written. "Great," she replied. "I need to talk to you, when can we get together?" he said. She said nothing back.

Elisa got in the car, off to see Anaïs. She'd be putting in extra hours, but that's how things went. She'd taken on the case as if it were her most important one. She'd shelve her freelance consulting, the outside work that occupied her evening hours: the work she'd lived for, her outlet since splitting up with Mateu. For quite some time she'd felt like working had given her life meaning, now more than ever. Anaïs's case… Like Elisa, she was separated and suffered from the prejudices of those around her. But Anaïs was being called mentally unsound. Where would all of this lead?

Elisa knew she wanted to follow through with her investigation but wasn't sure why. She'd always believed in the blurry limits of insanity, but this case wasn't like the others. Anaïs lived in poor conditions of her own choosing, and everything seemed to revolve around her activism. If it was purely activism, what the hell were she and the doctors doing there? Sitting at the wheel, Elisa hesitated to start the engine.

In the end, she did.

She left town, taking roundabout after roundabout as she passed between olive groves. The heat bore down on the dry afternoon landscape. She passed Vilarer on her left side, slipping into a land of farms and leafy vines that stretched out to Sant Jaume. A sea of green, she thought. She left her car near Quatrecases. The vineyards were twice as green as they had been on her last visit. Once more, her heels would have to take on the dirt trails, followed by the soft soil. She got out of her car, adjusted her short skirt and tights, grabbed the file and rested it on her waist. As she swung her hip against the car door to close it, she looked up to see several people from the neighbourhood whispering from their doors and stone entryways. She walked up the asphalt street that abruptly stripped down to a dirt road, dodging the sheep poop as best she could. The Twin Mountains were nearby, the air no longer disguising the scent of the farms, and she could make out Anaïs's stone hut, which crowned that far-off vineyard. She studied her surroundings in awe. A field below the sudden slope of two hugging mountains, close to the highway exit, soon to be smothered under buildings and roads for an unfettered warehouse complex. And the sheer difference it would make to its beauty. The whole thing was depressing. It was a place where, in other times, children would have missed school to gather grapes. Now she would never allow such a thing — it was banned. She wondered if those children had been happy there, then realised she didn't know, would never know, because she belonged to another time.

She was approaching Anaïs's vineyard. Everything was blanketed in green. Between the trees along the partition, she made out clothes that had been hung out to dry on a line connecting the stone hut to the almond tree. Shirts, shorts, underwear, socks… She'd arrived.

Anaïs stuck her head out of the doorway, her face pale. Her hair was damp from having just showered. She'd grown thinner since their last visit. She gave Elisa a defiant look, as if to say that she recognised her from the day she'd dragged her out, kicking and screaming, with the help of others from the medical team, and she asked her what she could possibly want now. Elisa put on a friendly, measured tone and asked for permission to come in. Anaïs let her in, though in obvious resignation. Pieces of pottery on the ground, dusty furniture, stone walls covered in cobwebs. She took down notes. She'd been curious about the clothing hanging outside, and when she asked if Anaïs could do laundry there, she replied that she did her laundry at home, which was only a mile and a half away, and then hung it out to dry in the vineyard. Although it seemed like she'd only answered that way to avoid pointing out the utter absurdity of the question. Elisa knew that her presence made Anaïs uncomfortable, but she persisted. She sat on Anaïs's bed because it was the only place to sit and then asked her why she hadn't wanted to meet at her office. "Because there's nothing wrong with me," Anaïs declared. And Elisa's eyes grew wide as she looked at the bed, then at the dirt floor and the surrounding walls. But Anaïs stood her ground. Elisa didn't back down, either, and she asked her to look around and ask herself if she thought that all of this was really normal. Then Anaïs said something that Elisa didn't know the answer to. She asked what "normality" meant to her, if her laws, which

Elisa knew really meant the laws of the system, changed as often as the tide. And so she, of course, changed the subject.

"What are you trying to achieve here?"

"To stop construction of the warehouse."

"And how will you manage to do that?"

"If I hold out here, they won't be able to destroy the shed."

"And what'll happen to the rest of the vineyard?"

"I have a plan."

"Which is?"

"I'm not telling you."

Elisa had picked up her pen to write everything down in her notebook, but Anaïs clammed up. Elisa stopped asking questions for a bit. She thought about the person in front of her, who obviously didn't trust her. But Anaïs had let her come in, sit on her bed, speak with her, which was a lot, given that they didn't know each other at all. She peered at the sky through the door and continued with the interview. She wanted to know what Anaïs had to say about Miquel.

He was a strange old man, Anaïs was saying. Then Elisa suggested that only Anaïs had seen him. But that wasn't true. Foix had seen him once and had drawn a picture of him, although Anaïs couldn't prove it because her daughter had taken him for her Great-Grandpa Pau. While she was explaining all that, Anaïs rummaged through the old drawers. Elisa kept writing in her notebook. That was new, Foix had also seen someone strange. Anaïs took out the wrinkled drawing she had spoken of, handing it over to Elisa. She took it and looked at it sceptically. Then, lifting her eyes from the page, Elisa told her that Magí and Jan believed that she'd imagined him, and asked how that made her feel. Anaïs, annoyance rising in her voice, replied that her father and Jan were the crazy ones. But Elisa wanted to keep insisting, touch upon every topic and take full advantage of the visit.

And what did she have to say about the pottery? Her brother and father also thought that she'd never be able to show proof of anything to stop the project. And what about the old trick for the rabbit problem? Anaïs kept disparaging her father and Jan, appearing tired and angry, and said that they didn't have a clue, that she didn't want to talk about it anymore, and for Elisa to go back to her office and leave her alone.

Elisa got up and went to the door.

"Are you going to make an appointment with the psychiatrist?"

"No."

"Will you take the medicine?"

"No."

"Will you come to my office?"

"No."

By the time she'd said goodbye, she'd already walked out the door and jotted down the last "No" in her notebook.

He saw Elisa coming down the road. He'd wanted to be there during her visit with Anaïs. It was too late. He'd wanted to explain everything he knew about the pottery and the old trick, even if they were insignificant details, but he hadn't dared. She made him nervous, and the closer she came, the more nervous he got. He asked her how Anaïs had looked as she passed him by, wanting her to say: "Don't worry, much better." But she didn't pay any attention to him. She cited her protocols while she kept on her way, heels clicking.

Without giving it a second thought, Jan grabbed her arm. He noticed that she didn't pull away — neither her gaze, nor her arm. Elisa let one of her hands go slack, holding the file in the other. And she didn't stop staring at him, in silence. Yes, that's what she was doing, he thought, because he hadn't seen her head turn away from his. And what he could see, he could also touch. He faced her with his eyes closed. In a fraction of a second. Letting go of all thoughts. And her lips were full. And her touch, damp. And her teeth like rocks corralling the waves. And the far-off barking and the smell of farms in the air and the sheep shit beneath their feet. Then *smack!* Elisa's folder hit the ground. But he continued to stand there with his eyes closed, imagining their tongues caught up in a dizzying spiral. He could feel her short black skirt pulling away from his navy-blue jeans. From that erection behind his zipper. Then he opened his eyes. Elisa's ponytail was no longer undone by his fingers running through her hair, as he'd imagined, but combed slick with her clips and hair tie intact. And Elisa's infuriated face moved away from his. And she was saying, "What are you doing? Why are you trying to kiss me? Who do you think I am? Why are your hands on my skirt? People's respect for me, my seriousness, my reports, Anaïs, the most peculiar case of my entire career..."

THE BEACH

He picked up the phone.

Judit wanted to see him.

A soft breeze combed Les Madrigueres from the dunes to the palm trees, from the path to the golden waves under the setting sun. Spring had settled in at the beach, bringing with it ideal measures of solitude and companionship. Still safe from the hordes of summer tourists, locals were strolling about and taking in the wafts of fresh air. The chalky path dazzled ahead, interrupted only by the far-off shadow of a passer-by with a dog kept on a tight leash. He left them behind. He walked on the sand beside the marsh, an intense green cloaking the dunes. The warmish water made up for a winter that had gone on for too long. Then he remembered that the place wasn't his. It belonged to them both. The memory of Samira unsteadied him as he walked along the water, making him recall the verse "to hear the faraway voice of the sea," which was the last thing he'd read before Anaïs had shut herself up inside the shed, leaving him and his father in charge of Foix. He sat sideways on the sand: the sea to his left, the dunes to his right. He turned his head from side to side, contemplating all that beauty as if he were looking for something within that undisturbed sliver of nature. The water wasn't ready for swimming yet. He contemplated its true size, motionless depth, colossal breadth. It'd been days since he'd last written to Samira. He didn't want to come across as needy. You couldn't tread the dunes if you wanted them to exist, if you wanted them to grow. Everything was empty and exquisite, like their last few days, or like days on the beach. And now there was Elisa.

As he traced the horizon, the shore and the path with his gaze, a woman who must have been Judit came into view — she wore a skirt above the knee and a denim jacket, walking all alone and staring out at the water. He waved his arms up and down so she could see him. It was her. She saw him and made her way towards him. She kept pushing down her skirt, which was flying up in the wind.

She struggled across the sand until she reached him. Then she sat down next to him, crossing her legs and stretching them out. Her legs pressed against each other, skin on skin. Smiles, hellos, a few jokes, a caress on the shoulder, how are yous. The water's surface began to swell with the rising tide. Judit stared at it, pulling her unbuttoned jacket closed with both hands to cover her chest.

"I can't get the other day out of my head," she said.

Jan rested his arms on his knees. He peered at her from the side of his eye in a panic, bringing his hands to his wrinkled forehead.

"It'd be best for that not to happen again," he said.

She asked why. He let out a tired sigh and said that his life was a mess. He looked out at the horizon, speaking so softly that he could barely hear himself, as if the sea were swallowing up his cowardly voice. He didn't quite know what to say. If he were to say the wrong thing, it'd be better for her not to hear him at all. She told him to leave it be, he'd said enough. She got up, accidentally flashing her underwear. Before she went back the way she'd come, she looked at him: if he ever felt like trying the whole attic thing again, he'd better not call.

But he didn't let her go. He felt lost and needed someone to talk to.

"What do you want to talk about? You're living a lie!" she said, her hair flying toward the dunes in the breeze while the sand blustered between her skirt. Jan didn't understand what she was talking about, but it was all very clear to her.

"You're a coward!"

Then she sat back down beside him, not worrying about her skirt this time. She'd called him a coward, and he didn't think she was wrong. Yes, of course he was scared. He was scared of losing her as a friend. They'd slept together. He was scared of losing Samira. She'd moved to Canada. He was scared of the rumours in town. Anaïs was at the heart of the gossip. He was scared of Elisa. She was looking into Anaïs's case, and he was attracted to this woman twice his age but he couldn't tell if it was sexual or what. He was scared of Anaïs. What would happen to Anaïs? What would Elisa do with Anaïs? What would happen to Foix? He was scared of the future. He wasn't in school, didn't have a job, and didn't have anyone to love.

"Fuck, I'm just lost!" he burst out, a tear in his eye as he looked out at the horizon.

Judit put her arm around him and leaned her head on his shoulder.

"It'll all work out," she said, looking him in the eye.

"You're a good friend," he smiled.

But then Judit's expression changed completely. It was as if those words had finished her off. As if a bucket of water from the deepest sea had been poured on her head. She was a good friend. Meaning she wouldn't be a good lover. To say one thing implied the other. Now he not only felt like a coward, but like an idiot, too. He could have waited a few days to tell her. There'd been no need for that; not there, not then. She was a good friend. And they wouldn't meet up in the attic anymore. Or call each other with veiled intentions. No making out, no his skin on hers. She was a good friend. And it was lucky that salty drops of water flashed in the wind, so that any tear trapped inside either of them would go unseen if it managed to escape. You're a good friend, too. Smiles. A kiss on one cheek, a kiss on the other. Goodbyes. Judit got up more elegantly than she had a few minutes back.

"By the way, do you know anything about rabbit repellents?" he asked, lifting his gaze while protecting his eyes from the round pumpkin sun hanging in the west.

"My grandfather used to scatter dog poop out in the vineyard," she replied, tugging at her skirt again. "But what do I know? That's what they did in the olden days, I think."

Judit buttoned up her jacket and got ready to go.

"And what about the rumours we talked about?" he asked, almost under his breath.

"Well, you said it yourself. They're rumours," she winked, turning on her heels to go back the way she'd come.

Jan watched her go. Samira had also heard of the rabbit trick. So they were wrong to think Anaïs had been making things up. Now Judit trudged along the sand, perhaps ruminating over his cowardice. He didn't want her to think of him that way. So he ran up to her. I'll walk you to your car.

After they'd crossed the empty path, she got in her car, fastened her seatbelt and said goodbye, hands on the steering wheel. Jan noticed that Judit still had sand on her shoes. She hadn't managed to brush it all off.

There was Jan, revving up the engine. There was the U-turn to Vilarer from the beach. There was the national road. The roundabouts pointing toward the sky. The olive branches pointing toward the earth, like trusting arms on a piggy-back ride. And the pottery, Samira, childhood, ancient tricks and secrets. There was Elisa's investigation into the case, and a few points that required clarification. There was Elisa, who'd think he was just making up excuses to get close to her instead of actually trying to convince her that the rabbit trick wasn't bullshit. It wasn't just Mohamed saying it; Samira said so too. And it wasn't just Anaïs saying it; Judit said so too. But Elisa would be sceptical, and he didn't know how to tell her. It would be hard to find the right moment.

There was the memory of that attempted kiss. There was his face in front of hers, Elisa's body, his body, his gaze — much too high a price to pay for words.

THE PLATFORM

The bulldozers would arrive in a week. The sky herded a few white clouds above the vines and trees — olive, almond, carob — that someone had planted in the earth and that someone else would now callously rip out. But a few white clouds wouldn't blot out the variegated light falling in every direction, from the Twin Mountains to Quatrecases, from Montmell to Castellot.

Carles and Marcel sat long-faced and silent in the Jeep, attempting to choke down their own powerlessness. Marcel, holding tight to his ecological convictions, commiserated with Carles as they passed the vineyard that had been purchased against his will, patting him on the back while he looked ahead. Carles had stopped tending his vines in anticipation of the coming construction. He explained everything fatalistically between puffs of the joint he held outside of the lowered window. Naturally, he'd accepted the settlement money. What else should he have done? Let them take everything while he just watched? Getting paid the appraised value was the bare minimum. As for the value of the land and the region and of humanity itself, he'd dedicated his precious time to fighting alongside the rest of the platform. No one could hold anything against Carles, not in the slightest, and Marcel understood him — the vineyard was his and he could do whatever he wanted with it, naturally. There was no way he could hold that against his friend.

Many of the members of the cellar co-op had been affected, but Magí's case had stunned everyone from the region and Penedès beyond. They'd only taken his small vineyard at the foot of the Twin Mountains, and he'd decided to refuse the settlement money, calling it a matter of dignity. How admirable! What a hero! But Carles wasn't so sure. Since when had Magí been such a fighter? News of the matter spread through the co-op, through all of Vilarer, like a plague of phylloxera. Carles knew Magí had refused the money because his daughter had asked him to, in honour of her grandfather. Marcel nodded his head in agreement. Carles was absolutely right, but there was no denying that *she* was one — a fighter. Nor would he deny that she was starting to lose it. In fact, that's why they were going to talk to her in the vineyard. They had to figure out what she was really proposing, to know first-hand why she was risking her father's pay out, understand what the hell she was doing between the four walls of that neglected stone shed and, above all, ask her to join forces with the platform. All of that militant potential, however obsessive, erratic and radical, needed to go toward supporting the organisation. Anaïs couldn't keep going at it alone. They had to tell her that so many others were of a similar mind, she had to know that. She had to join up with them and get behind the larger group's tactics.

The shepherd's flock, the landscape all around them and the unanswered questions surrounding Anaïs's behaviour provided enough fodder to avoid recognising the evidence of their defeat. Both Carles and Marcel had fully committed to the platform, but they saw their failure as the last stone of that slippery slope, that winding road covered in sheep shit, plastered under the wheels of their Jeep.

The sound of a car had Anaïs running towards the door, leaving behind a bowl of beaten egg and the asparagus she was sauteing over her little stove. Were her father and brother back to bother her? Or was it nosey Elisa? She stuck her head out of the half-open door just as the engine went silent and the handbrake screeched. She leaned against the stone wall, waiting to see who would climb out of the mysterious Jeep. After a few seconds she saw them: one of Vilarer's richest landowners and a vacationing yuppy from the region who'd just travelled the world on god knows how many planes. She knew they were part of the platform, but she didn't understand why they'd come over, given that they'd never see eye to eye with her on the efficacy of her bolder methods. She had no desire to work with that crowd, governed more by protocol and folkloric activism than clear, concise goals. The bulldozers would arrive in a week and she didn't have time to put up with people like them. She hoped to send them packing, despite the niceties that remained: their bothersome walk over, their heavy steps packing down the loose furrows beneath their feet, the predictably useless conversation, then their plodding back and the Jeep starting up all over again.

They went back with more to talk about than they'd come. Anaïs's proposal was even more surprising than they'd imagined. They couldn't join her in that act. No, they couldn't put so much at risk. They'd taken all the necessary steps to do it the right way, the peaceful way. They'd spoken with the mayors of all the affected towns, gathered a record-breaking number of signatures, held protests… They'd even blocked the national road on a busy Sunday afternoon. Their fight had brought all the people from the area together and been widely covered by the press. Even though they hadn't prevailed, they'd been very close to striking political deals to temper the magnitude of the project. Not to mention that no one could hold anything against the platform because they'd shown their full commitment. And Carles and Marcel were proud of that.

Anaïs would fight till the bitter end, but not them, because their fight was already over.

THE LAST DAY

The dark mountain summit fenced the sun in as Anaïs sat on the shed's doorstep, a deep sense of peace settling over her clouded mind. It was the night before the bulldozers would arrive. Her grandfather's tractor was parked by the stone partition, engine intact, its trusty plough having loosened the dirt and turned it into a cemetery of weeds. Leaves adorned the new vines and, hanging from the shoots, clusters of tiny xarel·lo grapes, untouched by the rabbits, were fighting to grow. In front of her, she saw the winding path leading up to the shed where she now sat in contemplation, and there, past the field and the stone partition, she could make out another vineyard, then another and another — a sea of green plots with no end in sight. On one side, Quatrecases marked the land's end, and above, ensconced and invulnerable, were the parcel vineyards. The Foix mountains stood seaside, and past them was the sea itself, a dreamscape beyond that northern land.

She had to go over her plan. Nobody at the platform would do anything bold. There'd been no shortage of protests, signatures, failed meetings with mayors... but nobody wanted to stop the equipment by force, and she sensed she was alone. They were all a bunch of cowards. She, however, was willing to put her body on the line.

Meanwhile Jan scrolled through the contacts on his phone as he sat at the bar in Fanal. He took a swig of beer. He didn't know whom to meet up with. Another swig. Migrated, married with children... Another swig. Not even the beer could get Elisa out of his head. Another. A woman almost twice his age had rejected him! Yet another swig. How many failures would it take for him to finally accept that Samira was gone? Another swig, hoping it would be the last. He was tired of crying. He asked the waiter for the bill, then left the bar and started walking. He lingered in front of Judit's front door. She'd installed an intercom to the attic. He rang. Judit asked, "Who's there?" And he said, "Judit, it's Jan." Silence. More silence. Jan didn't know if it was an empty or heavy kind of silence, or whether it would have a beginning and an end or only a beginning. Amid that uncertain wait, the intercom's droning static signalled an unlocked door.

It wouldn't be long before dark. As she smoked a cigarette out on the doorstep, she remembered that she'd usually see Miquel walking along the stone partition around that time. She'd look at him differently this time, as if he were her last hope during that night-long watch against destruction. Would he help her? Was he really an enemy? Maybe she'd been exaggerating, what with Foix's drawing and getting so worked up about protecting the stone hut and her collection… She needed someone else to help her stay inside the shed, even if they tried to demolish it with her inside. Someone would have to make sure that she'd be unable to leave no matter how hard she tried. He was the only person who could help her. "Yes!" she cried out. He was a true outsider and wouldn't mind binding her to the shed, and tightly so. Maybe he'd understand her mission and help her, either on principle or to win her over after all the scuffles they'd had over the last few months. But it was a bad idea anyway, asking a stranger to tie her hands up to a wall… But if she did, everyone would have to believe that Miquel wasn't a figment of her imagination after all. It'd mean she wasn't crazy. But now that she thought of it, if he put himself at risk for her, there was no way she could rat him out.

He walked up to Judit's attic. With every step, Elisa's silhouette sharpened in his mind. He recalled her legs as she bent down to pick her folder up from the ground. He recalled expecting an endless kiss, followed by the erection in his pants, and Elisa fixing her skirt while she declared that never in a million years would she be with him. The attic door stood ajar. He flung it open, walked in and shut the door behind him. He found himself unable to say anything to Judit. Hypocrisy is a coward's best friend. But he wasn't sure if he was staying quiet to keep himself from being even more of a hypocrite, or out of fear of being found out. It didn't matter. She'd let him in. She was there waiting for him, hair unkempt, in her loungewear. Their eyes locked and he pulled her close so that he wouldn't have to utter a word. They felt for one another hungrily. A strange wind nudged them toward the bed. They peeled off each other's clothes. He thought himself brave because he'd looked her in the eye — Elisa a sheer veil between them.

A soft light filtered through the walls, waking her from restless sleep. She got up quickly, threw on her clothes, flung open the rotting, wooden door and breathed in the dawn's serene blue. An imposing day was coming, one invulnerable to destruction. Yes, the sun would warm the grapes to make them grow, and the clouds had only cleared to ease the farmers' workday. No, she knew it: that day the sky would not invite destruction. Help was on its way, and soon everything will have been worthwhile. Maybe it would make a difference, resisting annihilation from inside that shed.

AND MAYBE I'M CRAZY

Tied up among the stones like a medieval prisoner or an animal roped to a tie-down ring with no opening like in the olden days and me standing here with my hands tied and the door closed so they can't see me when they start construction guaranteeing they'll tear it down with me inside the deed's already done and it'll all come crashing down on me yes oh yes and the bulldozer will arrive without seeing me and the stone hut will crush me but I'm doing it to save the vineyard because no one here wants to get their hands dirty but wait I still can't hear anything I still have time to think it over I can rest my head on the wall and stare at the cracks and the green of this spring against this unjust assault although it's hard so hard that no one wanted to stop it by force no one dared confront it head on no one was brave enough and I've got no choice but to resist with my whole self my body on the line in an act of resistance yes oh yes resisting from within the hut and I don't know if it's alright but I'm sure things will happen they'll be intense and extreme and brutal so they won't go on destroying this earth when the bulldozer has hurt me my body they won't be able to keep going no no not at all and I can't move I'm like a puppy and my puppy den is this dry-stone igloo and I can't leave and the time from right now until the machine comes will be the longest of the past few months and I see the cracks and I can see the grape leaves through the holes and I'm calm so calm because this was all I could do and everyone'll know it and respond you'll all see Anaïs take a deep breath Anaïs rest your head now that you can and look calmly through the cracks and remember everything you've done remember who you are and all that's happened that Grandma was widowed and then died and remember that September too its farming crisis and the harvesters going up in smoke that dawnless night and my uncle's a capitalist and my aunt's a gossip and the teenagers staring ahead like fish and Jan doesn't look like a fish but he's a lost boy from Neverland and my father has no feelings and as for my daughter I'm not sure what she thinks about the separation because even though I don't care everyone's whispering about it and there are rumours around town like the colours changing every year and scents of sun and moon but the harvest is dormant and the firewood's kindled and there are shops with wooden shutters and supermarkets open all day long and street corners with no kids on their bikes and abandoned farmyards and cats with nine lives and their old women who become eccentric yes eccentric like me but the firewood's kindled and its aroma is beyond compare and the breadth of the roads is eternal and I'm done designing and now I work the land and search for pottery and everyone speaks under their breath and maybe I'm a madwoman but I'll take the collection over to the historians and I'll stop the construction in the region and today I'll get hurt and then they'll have to stop and maybe I'm crazy but they want to ruin the landscape and life on earth because they aren't listening to the platform or the birds or the people and I can hear the danger because the sound of an engine is drawing closer yes yes yes it's here I can hear the bulldozer ripping out the vines on the far side of the vineyard although this wall and these ropes that I'm straining with my wrists like a medieval prisoner or animal won't let me see I can't see through the holes in the door because I'm tied up too tight but it's all the same nothing's happening they won't cross the hut with me inside because after maiming me or killing me they won't be able to keep going but the bulldozer is the kind that kills and serves and betrays as if their value weren't coming from the earth itself as if they had no land and the citizen's platform is full of cowards but I've cared for the vines and my grandfather is thanking me from wherever he is and it'll all bite the dust with the bulldozer but the land is work and value and strength and everyone's crazy and I'm putting up a fight here but the rest of them are cowards and they forget the corriol de Santa Maria de Foix and the River Foix that traces Penedès beyond the rolling mountain ranges and they dismiss the trick with rabbit poop as if nature could create the smell of bleach but there are some helpers like that old man that oh so mysterious man whom no one knows and no one's ever seen apart from me and the shed is like a house with a messy dirt floor and scattered pottery and the mattress and sheets and furniture and tools and canned food and a portable stove and the tractor and the plough but I can hear the danger because there's the sound of an engine that isn't a tractor no and the light of dawn races toward morning like a hare now wait I can also hear my daughter's shouts but shit shit shit I don't understand but how can this be but why but who can tell me why I'm hearing my daughter's shouts amid the sounds of an engine if that wasn't part of the plan damn it holy fuck but in the end it's true that each voice belongs to someone and there's no doubt that Foix is on the other side of that door.

THE BULLDOZER

"What are you doing here?" Anaïs asked in a gravelly morning voice. "You need to leave right now. You could hurt yourself!" she said. But her little girl wasn't paying any attention to her. She simply walked in and shut the door. She squinted as she said, "Mama, I miss you." "But why didn't you go to school?" Anaïs asked. "Uncle Jan was gone today." "Are you serious?" "I promise." "Then listen to me," Anaïs said, motioning with her head to call her in closer. Her daughter walked toward her, perplexed by the ropes, her tied wrists and that metal ring. "You have to get out of here, right now," Anaïs said. They looked each other in the eye. "Why?" the girl asked, still staring at the ropes, a tear catching the light from a crack between the stones. "Because I said so!" Anaïs's furious cries were like rocks pummelling down a mountain slope. "I don't want to leave!" "Get out of here, dammit!" A merciless hailstorm. And then Foix calmed down and asked what they'd done to her and why she was all tied up. Anaïs gave up. "Come, Foix, come here. Untie this rope. I'm getting you out of here myself."

He opened his eyes. The attic ceiling bled into dream. Then he remembered Fanal Bar, the staircase, Elisa's tormenting rejection, Samira like a perpetual star... And the open door. Judit. Their embrace. That moment. Forgetting it all. A night long and slender as a vine in the harvest. And the billowing sheets. That high window — a hidden refuge like the lookout point at the hermit chapel. And merciless sex gliding over his memory like a horse leaping over a paddock. Sex like a runaway horse. A body the colour of honey stretched out under him like a dusty road. The pillow where he'd always reminisce about that night. While last night seemed to have happened for no good reason. Because from up there, in the attic, where the malicious stares of Vilarer couldn't pierce him, all he wanted was to see Samira. Not Judit, not Elisa. Neither of them. And he looked at the honey-coloured body sleeping beside him like a still rooftop. Judit was like a rooftop. And he was like water gushing from a drainpipe.

Foix tried to untie the rope tangled around the metal ring and Anaïs's wrists, culminating in a few thick, dusty knots. The fine skin on her little hands — skin of Anaïs's skin — took on an uncertain feat. The bulldozer pulled closer. Anaïs knew it because of the rumble; her breath quickened, and she thought about how on earth she'd got to that point. Foix was nearly panting from trying to unfasten the knot. Anaïs forgot all about the leaves, roots, vines, branches and grapes and about the tractor too, because the only thing she wanted then was for her arms to be free to pick up her daughter, hold her firmly, place her on her back and get on out of there.

Judit opened her eyes. Jan smiled. Judit smiled too. The colour of honey. A pillow that no longer existed. His thoughts gone too. There were but two lips, a shy kiss, two breasts against one chest, and four legs wrapped into one. There was the high window, the street that was too far down, a distant Samira, a forgotten Elisa. There he was, like water gushing from a rooftop drainpipe after a storm. Two breasts against one chest, two legs in the air and a horse with no paddock. Lips, teeth, hills and waves. Up and down. Nothing else. Shit, Foix, he thought. He stilled the waves and looked her in the eye, as if pleading for forgiveness. He drew back slowly but without hesitation. Shit, Foix, he thought again. There was a watch. There was his jumping out of the bed, underwear turned inside-out, the sleep in his eyes, his T-shirt tag out front. There was a rush down the steps, the front door and his undone zipper. But there was also Foix, forgotten. And shit, shit, it was the 30th of May.

While the engine grew louder, Anaïs shut her eyes, imagining the pristine vines vanishing beneath the bulldozer. Years quashed by a machine, like grapes falling down the chute in the wine cellar during the harvest. A year's work released from the trailer in a booming rush. The tables had turned, like diving into a wave only to be sent rolling in the surf. In September, grapes are poured into the chute to continue the cycle, but now another kind of machine was guzzling up the vineyard to put an end to everything. While she thought about that, Foix kept trying to untie her but couldn't. The roar of the engine came closer still, so much so that Anaïs started calling out to the workers in the cabin — she would never forgive herself if Foix were to get hurt. But the roar was as loud as her cries or louder still, so Anaïs said, "Go, Foix, leave right now," but she refused to do as she was told. The machine wasn't stopping, and it was already there, very close. Foix didn't want to leave, she just didn't, and Anaïs didn't know if it was due to her being scared or out of love or simply because she couldn't understand what was happening. The little girl couldn't understand, of course not. She was just a child. Maybe she didn't need to understand, but at that moment, she must have felt the desperation. One end of the shed started to shake, and Foix's ear-splitting shriek pierced the air right as a wall came tumbling down, a few stones from the ceiling crashing down, too. Then, right after that transcendent cry, the machine pulled to a stop.

Half of the stone hut had been destroyed. Foix huddled up and cried in the corner left most intact, burrowing her head under her arms. Her sobs seemed timid, lost. Anaïs's hands were tied, her head bloody from a few falling stones. The bulldozer operator, perplexed, instinctually opened up the glove compartment. His knowing fingertips moved on their own account once he pulled out his mobile.

After he'd made the call, he climbed down from his machine and tried to untie her, but the ropes were too tough. He went and got a water bottle, told her not to worry and that the ambulance and the police were almost there, then poured water on her wounds. He gave the little girl a tissue, and tried to calm her down, saying everything would be okay very soon. Before long the police, doctors and nurses trekked up the path. Anaïs muttered that they could go right ahead but that nobody was getting her out of the shed. That nobody should even think about touching her. Because the construction could not proceed. She'd be there to stop them till the very end.

An ambulance followed by two police cars unsettled the landscape. The road to Quatrecases had been cut off, but Jan and his father were allowed to pass. Jan didn't want to get lost in the details. Too much had happened that neither of them understood. Foix had been in danger, Anaïs had put herself at risk… But this was no time for pointing fingers. Anaïs had tried to stop the construction — and she'd succeeded. She'd never reveal who had tied her up, and the police said that they had to conduct a proper investigation. They needed time to collect evidence. There was no going back. She'd managed to stop the construction in the region for an entire day. Jan couldn't get that out of his head. It was one day, but that was plenty. He thought about how that single day would come to mean a great deal. About how it had better be long and beautiful. He thought that someone had to make sure it lasted, so that the days to come would be just like that one. His sister had stopped the construction. Just like she'd warned them. Was it true that there was still hope? Had she been right all along? They had to make the most of that moment. Stopping the construction for a day was not enough. Now they had to stop time. He hadn't yet reached Llobeta Vineyard — where besides police cars and ambulances there was also a small plot of upturned vines, and another nearby plot where they'd torn up some more — when he rang up Marcel from the citizen's platform and said that they needed to call a meeting that very night.

WHITE COAT

Anaïs saw a white bed, four white walls and people dressed in white. She curled her legs up under the sheets and wondered what she was doing there, why she wasn't at home, close to her daughter, her land, her vineyard, her shed filled with junk and neglected tools. But she didn't see anything she recognised. Only a white bed, four white walls and people dressed in white. A stout man and a lanky young woman came into view as she blinked. For a moment, she thought it was a dream. Her vision was blurry. She heard strange voices. She remembered the ambulance that had left her then gone. Maybe it had gotten mixed up in the bustle of the city, which was so different from the peace of Vilarer. The voices said that they didn't want to hurt her, but she thought that if they didn't want to, that meant they still could. The voices kept talking. Don't worry, take a deep breath, the police aren't here any longer. The sedatives will kick in, in a minute.

But what sedatives were they talking about? Startled, Anaïs sat up. The large man, frowning though he spoke in a kind, measured voice, told her that she'd started kicking at anyone who tried to untie her hands. But she was only defending her land — this she said firmly — then the young woman intervened, reminding her that she'd also said she'd been tied up of her own free will. Anaïs changed the subject — her back didn't hurt anymore, her head had been stitched up, meaning she could go home now, thank you very much. She made to get up and leave, but the woman held her back from the right side of the bed: the nurses had already tended her wounds hours ago. And beforehand, in the ambulance, added the man from the other side of the bed. So what was she doing there? The man sat down on the bed and looked Anaïs in the eye. We're not in an ordinary hospital, Anaïs. Well, then, where are we?

Jan imagined Anaïs waking up and realising that she was in a psychiatric ward. He imagined a scream flooding the room, moving through the hallway, up the stairs then out to the neighbourhood and city. Like when they were little, when they'd scream from opposite sides of the pathway lining the vineyard. Jan didn't know what the hell was going on in that faraway medical centre, but he felt like Anaïs was crying out, like her screams were bouncing off the walls, back at him, helpless as he was in Vilarer, seized by the echo of the Twin Mountains that cradled Llobeta Vineyard. His father was sitting on the couch. Elbows on his knees. Palms on his forehead.

"Elisa just called," his father said without looking up. "Get this! She does me the kindness of checking in while Foix's father won't even pick up my calls, the deadbeat…"

"He still doesn't know what happened?" Jan asked.

"No…" his father looked up to gesture at the phone, "I'm telling you, kid, he's not answering!" And he put his hands back on his forehead.

"What did Elisa want?"

"The court asked for an urgent report on Anaïs, and she has 48 hours to write it. I'm not completely sure of all she said. It seems like the police, or the doctors, or someone — she's not sure who — reported the incident to the Public Ministry for Minors. Because Foix was in the shed, goddamit!" With each new piece of information he gestured wildly with one hand, resting his head on the other. "This time she's really put her foot in it."

"What are you saying?" Jan, distraught, took two steps backward and slammed his back into the kitchen door.

"Don't you get it?" His father stood up, animated, and walked toward him. "The situation was out of hand; you know that better than anyone. She was close to getting herself hurt, and getting Foix hurt, too! She was showing signs of psychotic, or neurotic, behaviour or whatever you call it, when the police and the EMTs stepped in. The doctor ordered that she be admitted straightaway, and we don't know how long she'll need to stay in that goddamn medical centre. Everything's gone too far… it's even reached the courts! We've got to let the people who know what they're doing do their jobs, son. Or do you want Foix to really get hurt next time?"

"But, Dad… Foix was there by accident… it was my fault, actually. I didn't take her to school on time."

"It's all the same, kid. Anaïs went and did something nuts!" and he banged his fist against the door. "I've had it! First her obsession, then the fire, then the faeces and now she locked herself up in the shed."

"But, Dad… You don't know everything…"

"What is it that I don't know?"

"The trick to get rid of the rabbits… It was real, some folks from around town said so."

"It doesn't matter, things have gone too far."

"I'm not finished! Anaïs has been collecting pieces of pottery for twenty years now. Samira and I found them in the shed when we were little."

"And what do you mean by that?"

"That it's not just a sudden obsession, but more of a secret hobby."

"So why didn't you say all of this at Elisa's office?"

"I don't know, I don't know! These little details are just, who knows… And that woman… she makes me nervous."

His father's phone rang. It was the psychiatric hospital. Anaïs was calmer now. She needed to stay for a few more days so they could diagnose her if they observed anything serious. Then Jan felt the pressing need to tell the people in the hospital that they didn't know the whole story. He felt it was his job to bombard them with everything he'd learned. He snatched the telephone out of his father's hands and his words overflowed like a raging river. Not being able to drown out his own grovelling tone because they had to know that Anaïs wasn't crazy. She wasn't. His father thought so, but it wasn't the truth. What was madness anyway? The word that a doctor had written in a file so that Anaïs would be committed? The things Elisa imagined from her office? The fantasies he'd had of Elisa and him? His father's preaching as he pumped his fist in the air when he talked about Anaïs? The man on the phone had to know that nothing was actually going on. Nothing. There was only a place, and that place had a past. There was a marital separation that was by all turns normal, and anyone who didn't think so was an idiot. There was a collection of pottery started with a cool, calm head, curiosity in full bloom with a bright future ahead. There was a trick to ward off rabbits that resurfaced by word of mouth. There was a threat and resistance. There were prejudices. And people who walked in flocks. Like sheep.

"It appears you've had to process some very strong emotions today," the interlocutor responded.

"What's that supposed to mean?" Jan said.

"Why don't you calm down some, rest a bit and let us do our jobs."

She had to see Anaïs. She'd received the court petition via fax. Now she only had two days to respond, in writing, with everything she knew about Foix and Anaïs.

In her miniskirt and low-cut shirt, a briefcase propped against her waist, she headed toward the mental-health centre, feeling the city open up before her, a place where she could be a nobody. Not a single passer-by would look at her pryingly. No one would care about her existence. Nor was there anyone around who knew that Anaïs existed, or that she was lying in a bed, against her will, on the second floor of a building downtown. But the doors to the centre, the supervised entrance, the white and the grey, would offer her their sincerest welcome. Inside the building, of course, everyone from the concierge to the psychiatrists knew who Elisa was.

Despite her twenty years of experience, she felt unsteady as she entered the building. She did not believe herself deserving of such respect because she respected no one in return. Where did they hide their stories, these transient walls? Where did they hide the joys and pains that travelled through each cry and kick and diagnosis? How to accurately measure the influence of culture on collective wellbeing, on our minds, our professions, our dreams, on every person's secret and not-so-secret impulses? Then she felt the urge to go back to the stone hut. She didn't understand anything in the city. But in the stone hut, the place itself stood in for words, while a single gust of wind could do away with her portfolio and documents.

Anaïs seemed calm enough. Elisa told her so, saying that she looked relaxed and serene, and that she was glad to see her that way. Anaïs replied that it was all the pills' doing, what else? But she was nicer than last time. Of course, she thought, she had to suck up to her. Anaïs was probably wishing with all her might for Elisa to write up a favourable report, and that was why she was being nice. But Elisa didn't care — she had a thick skin. Everyone wanted something from her. Elisa was there because she wanted something, too; there were no two ways about it. She'd cash her check at the end of the month. She wanted to know things, fill up her notebook, solve the most puzzling case of her career as rigorously as possible.

Elisa said she'd heard that Anaïs had gotten worked up that day. But a bulldozer was uprooting her life. But she'd kicked several police officers. But they were stronger. Who had tied her up? She wouldn't say. Why had she wanted to be tied up? To stop the construction. But…they'd resume the construction the next day… They wouldn't. How did she know? She simply knew, that's all. What did she mean? That the citizen's platform would do something about it. And if the construction stopped, would she go back to her normal life? Yes, she swore, and said that Elisa had to get her out of there no matter what. But it wasn't up to her, whether she got out or not. It was up to the doctors, the diagnosis and the situation. Anaïs had to understand that. Was Elisa sure she couldn't do anything about it? Okay, maybe she could offer her opinion on the matter, but that wouldn't do much… A judge wanted to know how Foix was doing, and that was Elisa's top concern. But she wasn't crazy, she wasn't! And she became agitated, as if the pills had worn off. So what did she have to say about Foix? That she would never forgive herself. The girl had come there on her own and Anaïs had tried to make her leave, but she hadn't managed in time. That it was her own fault for having abandoned her. And she swore she'd go back home to her design studio and her daughter.

Elisa wrote everything down, word for word, then left the room. In the elevator, she was still jotting down snippets of their conversation from memory. She walked past the lobby and barely nodded goodbye to the concierge. The story made sense. Anaïs had been clear and had made a commitment. But what about the pottery collection, the dog poop and her imaginary friend? Miquel, was it? Yes, that was his name, she leafed back through her notebook to check, coming to a stop as she left the centre, propping the door open with her elbow. Then she walked up the road, lost in thought. A sudden obsession, an unhygienic practice, a hallucination… Some of these things concerned the psychiatrist, but some were up to her. There was no end to this story, it seemed.

Once she got to El Vendrell, before reaching her office, she stopped at a Pakistani-run corner store in the tiled town square. She bought a jar of hummus, a pack of breadsticks and an apple. She didn't know how long she'd be in the office, or if she'd visit other patients when she was done. Anaïs's case had to be resolved quickly. That morning there'd been an incident — a psychotic episode, or maybe a spat of neurosis or something. Whatever it was, there'd been a judge's petition and a mental-health-centre admission. She chucked the food into her bag, crossed the tiled square and climbed up the stairs to her office. The administrator had already gone home. Her office was empty and dark. The afternoon waned and she hadn't eaten lunch. The pigeons were calm. She let herself drop onto the rolling chair, exhausted, pushing against the table so that she'd roll all the way to the balcony. Dipping the breadsticks in her hummus, she peered down at the street below. She was beginning to relax when the telephone rang.

"Social Services. How may I help you?"

"Hi, Elisa. It's Jan."

"Hi, Jan…"

"Did you get a petition from the court?"

"Yes."

"And what are you going to do?"

"I'm writing a report. I have to."

"Before you do anything, you have to hear me out."

"I've already told you I have to stay neutral."

"But listen, please."

"Okay, I'm listening."

"I didn't know whether to call you or come…"

"And why didn't you come?"

"It's just that when you're in front of me…"

"Jan, please, not again…"

"I wanted to say that…maybe Anaïs *is* making a big deal out of everything, but she isn't crazy!"

"What's changed?"

"The bags of dog poop."

"What about them?"

"She didn't make them up. It's a trick from the olden days."

"So she was right after all?"

"I only just learned about it!"

"Well, aren't *you* the farming experts?"

"Don't laugh, times have changed…"

"I'm sorry. Heh, heh!"

"Plus, her pottery collection isn't just a sudden whim."

"So you're a psychologist now?"

"Anaïs started her collection when she was twenty years old. I saw it myself when I was little."

"And what about Miquel?"

Jan fell silent. But he had said a few interesting things. She hung up the phone and when she finished jotting everything down, she grabbed the apple, curled up in the chair and looked out at the street as she took her first bite. Anaïs was putting the shards of pottery to use in a struggle that she couldn't explain with words alone because it was rooted in the vineyard's ancient past. She couldn't write the word *passion* in a social-services report. Or *memory*. Or *cultural heritage*. But she had to take in the landscape so that she could assess it all, then find the right word. A *connection*, perhaps? But this was about the people, not about a single person and her land. She had to go there. She was bending the rules, but first the flesh-and-bone Elisa had to get it, and then the thick-skinned Elisa might understand it too. She had to go back to the stone hut, even if there was no one there to see. Anaïs had been driven — and explosively so — to save the shoots on the vine. No matter if she smelled or filled her home with filth. No matter if her child had to play among bags of dog poop. No matter if nobody used that old trick anymore. Of course, now it made more sense. She was saving the vineyard, like they always had, because they'd all had to help out and pick grapes for the cycle to continue.

Several vineyards had bulldozers rammed into them like statues, some parts of the vineyards were already destroyed. She'd heard that the workers didn't have the green light to keep going until the day after, even though the police had collected enough evidence in a single morning. She meandered along the stone partitions and slender summer shoots that shuddered in the wind. There were a few brown stains against the infinite green — the construction had started that morning. And that's when she thought of all the families that went in and out of her office every day. They were labelled "unstructured." As if they didn't have a structure of their own. Maybe they'd simply been destroyed. But they wanted to live. So they would go to her office, looking for an answer. That earth couldn't walk or talk. Someone had to do it for her.

She was getting close to Llobeta Vineyard. As she trekked up in her heels, the stone hut came in and out of sight among the carob, almond and olive trees beside the partitions separating the estates. And then she caught a glimpse of a beret among the leaves of the carob tree that grew along the partition. Then she saw some espadrilles under the branches. And the closer she got, the clearer the beret and espadrilles — belonging to God knows who — came into view. The man was there, standing before the stone hut, his gaze fixed on the buried rubble. Elisa started to leaf through her portfolio and pulled out Foix's drawing, then she looked at the man, then back at the drawing, then back at the man.

"What's your name, ma'am?" he asked. And she stumbled over her name as she hastily tried to stash the drawing away in the portfolio she was balancing against her leg. "And you?" she asked, edging toward him, intrigued. "Miquel, at your service." She was speechless. She realised that he must have caught on to her astonishment. He looked at her, seemingly bewildered, from the side of his eye, refraining from turning his body away from the shed, as if he were standing in front of a warm campfire. "You look like you've seen a ghost!" "My goodness," she replied. Then he said not to worry, that he knew Anaïs spoke poorly of him, painting him as an intruder on account of her not knowing who he was. So she didn't know who he was. Meaning that he was someone whom very few people around these parts would recognise, and that there must have been a reason for it. So who could he be? And how did he know that Elisa knew Anaïs?

"I figured as much, seeing you here with a portfolio... especially today. I'm from Sant Sadurní. I have a home there, as well as a few cava cellars. Do you like cava?" He didn't wait for her to respond. "Hell, people don't drink wine every day like they used to!"

And what was he doing, standing there?

"Many years ago, I went to the Vilarer co-op on business. I was all about business back then. I was a grown man and never wished to marry. They'd call me…an eternal teenager!" What started as a chuckle broke into a loud cough. "Anyway, as I was saying, at the co-op, I met Anaïs's grandmother. Have you heard of Selma? I saw her climbing down from the tractor that her husband, Pau, drove, and she came running to the scale room where I was talking to one of the people in charge, then announced the grape variety they'd just brought over to the mill. It was xarel·lo. I saw her there, uttering that word, and I remember it as if it were yesterday." Miquel fell quiet, turning his attention from Elisa to the horizon. "She couldn't stand strangers trespassing on her land either. Sometimes I think Anaïs is a lot like her. She must have gotten in that same habit as a child, when she and her grandmother would walk these paths hand in hand, searching for snails after the rain or for asparagus in the spring."

Why was he telling her all this?

"Because one day she brought me here to the shed, you see? But when we came out of the hut she told me that she had a husband and children and grandchildren and land."

Elisa sensed that Miquel wasn't really talking to her any-more; he'd been set in motion and there was no stopping him.

"If you ever come around here, you'll find that there's a bridge that crosses over some train tracks at Sant Sadurní, right by Freixenet, at the outskirts of the wine cellars, over where the workers use acid to tint the bottles green. If you ever talk to any of those workers, they'll tell you that they often see people jumping off the bridge, killing themselves. But no one knows about this because the train operator will only announce "an incident" on the megaphone, as it doesn't sound right to say that some people just can't go on, you know? The world would have to stop turning. We can give thanks that the rail company says anything at all, because the television won't air it, not with one excuse or the other," said the man, pointing left and right with his cane.

"One day I put one leg over the edge. But before I got the other leg over, I saw Selma running across the bridge. I can't remember if I was wicked enough to call her and announce that I was going to kill myself, or if I'd asked her to come and see me and was cruel enough to put one leg over the edge. I only remember her worried face as she ran up to me on the bridge. She said she couldn't come with me, and again, she told me that she had a husband and children and grandchildren and land. But she said she'd never forget me. That she'd always hold me in her memory. I swung my leg back around. I didn't see her again until Pau's burial, almost twenty years later. I know she saw me. I know she must have been overcome with anxiety, but I hope she understood that I only wanted to be there, that was all. When I found out that she'd died of old age, I came back here, to the hut, to remember her. And I found someone just as obstinate about this here land."

Had he been the one to tie Anaïs up to the hut that morning? A spark of curiosity shone through her eager voice.

Miquel didn't answer the question but asked that she not tell his story to anyone. Once he said so, he fixed his eyes on the stone hut, as if saying goodbye, and parted like he was leaving behind a warm fire. He wound down the corriol de Santa Maria de Foix and camí de Pi de Llobets, his pace slow, his back hunched.

Elisa stayed there, thinking that she wouldn't be able to write that down in her report. No one would know of Miquel's story because that's what he'd asked of her. In any case, including the sad story of a third party she'd run into by chance wouldn't add anything of value to her report. She already knew that she'd strayed from the rules, making all kinds of strange things prone to happen. No one would know that she'd visited the stone hut without an appointment, as if she'd just been out for a walk in the countryside, wandering this way and that with the sole purpose of gathering notes on geology, instead of on Anaïs. It'd be unthinkable to tell a soul about it. She'd risk her reputation! And she had to consider her career. But now it all made more sense. The land…yes, the land…the story of that man whom everyone believed to be a figment of Anaïs's imagination had opened her eyes like the sun pries open the earth upon drying it. Now she only needed to write that damned report, and find the goddamn words for it.

THE DEMO

The day after the incident, there was Jan, the dark road, the balaclava and the headlamp. There was the corner of carrer de Dalt, his father, Mohamed, his cousin Jaume and even his cousin Víctor, whom he'd gotten to put down his game controller and go to the meeting the night before. There was no sign of Uncle Xavier or Aunt Empar, whom he hadn't convinced, or Judit, whom he wanted to believe stayed home because she was a conformist and not because she was upset with him, or Carles, who'd already taken the money and wouldn't allow himself to be seen at another one of these meetings. There was Marcel, who wouldn't dream of missing a brush-up. There were men and women approaching, trickling out into the darkness of the streets little by little. Then in groups.

There were bulldozers tucked between the vines like statues. There was an inky dawn, like the ocean. There were vines on the verge of ruin that needed to be saved by everyone who'd come out that early morning. And Anaïs locked up in that psychiatric hospital for having tried in the first place. There were many, many people all at once. There were knives, nails, drills, hammers and shears. There was the whole Quatrecases neighbourhood, their lights guiding them: the moon, the headlamps and the stars. There was a path, dark as a cave, but there were lots of people, and they were sticking together. There was the sound of crickets, dogs and farms. There was still life in that place. There was still life to take in.

There was an eerie silence and a hurried march forward together in the dark, in the shadow of the trees beneath the moon, the sound of a wild boar escaping along the partition as they passed. There were huge, thick tires, steel plates, glass and metal. It stood in yellow, but the night was black. There was the loud, heavy sound of a drill boring into a tire. There was a hammer, smashing things to pieces in the cab. There were nails and shears deflating *all* the tires. There was a hammer, then another, breaking the ignition, the steering wheel and the rear-view mirror. But nothing would happen. No one would punish them because they weren't anyone at all. They were legion, in the darkness. They were the people — no name, no face, no house. Only a place. No one in their right mind would mess with them. No one in their right mind would dream of touching any of them. If you messed with one, you messed with them all. There was Anaïs locked up in a psychiatric hospital for wanting to stop the bulldozers, so there had to be a great many of them to finish the work she'd started. They had to do incredible things, monumental things, to show that anything and everything was possible. There was the gentle sound of the tires deflating. There were the hammers smashing the glass, the levers, the buttons and everything that crossed their path.

There were the days that passed and brand-new bulldozers ready to start again. There were a thousand people of all ages from the entire region who, early in the morning, came to put their bodies on the line. They'd left at dawn, and the men and women had approached the meeting place, coming out of the darkness of the streets little by little and then in groups. There were vines that'd been saved twice over, once again on the verge of ruin, but everyone had come out one more time. And Anaïs was still locked up in the hospital. There were many, many people all over again. There were the workers, who were trying to do their jobs, the people who wouldn't move, and the workers who, once again, had to stop. There were the police, who attempted to intervene among people whose names and faces they didn't know, the people who wouldn't budge, and the police again, discovering the crowd was far too thick with bodies. No single person was the leader. Everyone was out in front; everyone was in the back. Everyone was a grandparent; everyone, a child. Everyone a woman; everyone a man. Everyone surrounded the machines, everyone stormed the streets and vineyards. The people had come from Vilarer and Sant Jaume, from all the towns in the region, from the beach, the Foix River and the mountains.

There was the passing day, the next arriving and people returning. There was all that had happened the day beforehand, now repeating itself like a rewound movie. And the next day. And the next and the next. Everyone was the same, with people who looked the same day after day. Even though they all had things to do. Despite the children having school. Everyone was there to finish the work that had been started. To pass on the landscape to their kids and grandkids, to their great-grandchildren and great-great-grandchildren. Every one of them was the leader. No one person stood in the back or out in front; they were all circles surrounding the machines, storming the roads and vineyards. No one was a grandparent and no one was a child: they were a united front. They were the people, no name, no face, no house. Only a place. Everyone but the people who believed in the Logistics Centre. Those who embraced the logistics boom and international commerce. Those who saw it as a way to end that never-ending unemployment. Everyone but Anaïs, who was still in the hospital against her will. There were the police, desperate, and the workers, the corporation and the government, who were beginning to understand that something was going on. There were the regions' mayors, who met with the government. And the construction that, according to them, would need to be paused for a while, maybe a few months, a year at worst, until the town had cooled off and forgotten about the whole matter…

Convinced that she'd saved the landscape from needless annihilation for some time to come, Anaïs let the satisfaction of having won that small battle sink in. But she dealt the cards over a white table, between four white walls, feeling somewhat indifferent about whether she'd win or lose. She dealt the cards but it wasn't for solitaire this time — Paula was nice enough, and they'd struck up a friendship. Paula was as thin as a reed, with one arm as pale as her face and the other covered in vibrant tattoos. She'd told her that she had three children, each with a different father, and that each of these fathers had really laid into her. That was all Paula would talk about. She never said why she was at a psychiatric hospital. Because, to her, those three fathers were the problem. And that's when Anaïs understood why everyone had gotten so worked up over her ex. It was that he had treated her well, of course. Maybe that wasn't the norm, for a man to treat a woman well, so she owed him her eternal gratitude. That explained it. While she noticed that she was earning more time at the game room by the day, she grew increasingly aggravated at everyone for keeping her inside. She'd been locked up for three weeks already. Was that the price she had to pay for her land? Had prolonging the vines' existence for a few scant months cost her freedom? She listened to words. Words and more words that weren't saying anything at all. They kept saying that none of it had to do with the vineyard, that she'd kicked the police... She'd even had to give a statement in court, since the Public Ministry for Minors wanted to know how Foix was doing, though of course the whole family had said that her daughter was fine. And Elisa, what might Elisa have said? They'd harped on about her unchecked obsession with her imaginary friend... How come this so-called Miquel hadn't gone to see her at the psychiatric centre? they'd asked. She wouldn't have wanted him to visit anyway, since the investigation around who had tied her up to the shed was still ongoing. Perhaps she'd never be able to prove that Miquel was more than a figment of her imagination. But how come no one else had ever seen him? What was he hiding from, this strange man? Why had he helped tie her up? Maybe she'd never know that either.

The room then the stairs, the elevator then the bay window, the sitting room and that companion, friend, inmate, loon or whatever she was supposed to call her. Everything was white. The white made everything cleaner, less crazy. But she kept turning everything over in her head. The room then the stairs, the elevator then the bay window, the sitting room and that companion, friend, inmate, loon or whatever she was supposed to call her. The woman's name was Paula. Her name was Anaïs. They both had a name. But everything was white and kept turning in her head. The room then the stairs, the elevator then the bay window, the sitting room and that companion, friend, inmate, loon or whatever she was supposed to call her. And what was *she* supposed to be called, as she kept turning things over from inside that white and grey building, locked up and far away, while someone else decided what to call her, what to call what she'd done, and what was going on inside her head. Anaïs ruminated on all that while she half-heartedly played cards, which meant that Paula would win. And that's when she thought that, if she was there, playing cards as if nothing were happening, without lifting a finger while everyone else judged her love for the land, then something strange was going on indeed. Maybe it was true, then — that she was crazy. Of course, she'd lost it, that went without question. That's why everything was white, and that's why she was going along with playing cards as if nothing had ever happened. That's why there was the room then the stairs, the elevator then the bay window, the sitting room and that companion, friend, inmate, loon or whatever she was supposed to call her. That's why all of these things strung together day after day like a welcome routine. How come her father hadn't done anything about it, or her brother either? That's when she understood. The cards shifted between the table and their fingers and the drawer and that hand's inertia, the elevator going up and down between schedules and visits and walks, the white ceiling spinning in circles between the white walls over a white bed for every night of that strangest of summers. That's the shape lunacy took — that was its colour, of course.

Two of coins, three of cups, five of wands... Then a nurse interrupted their hand to say that a lawyer was there to see her. The nurse accompanied her to the visitors' lounge, then he left her alone with him. He'd brought a letter from the court where she'd been summoned to answer some questions a couple of days ago. Anaïs didn't know where to start deciphering that jumble of large and small fonts before her. And then she saw it. She saw it and that was that, without having read the letter in any particular order. The case had been dismissed. She asked what that all meant, her voice shaking. The lawyer said that nothing had been the matter with Foix, that the investigation had been expedited because of the May 30th incident, but that all the reports and declarations on the situation had been favourable. Anaïs couldn't believe her ears. Elisa had ended up writing a favourable report after all. What a strange woman Elisa was. Never in a million years did Anaïs think Elisa would help her escape that nightmare.

They'd said she was a good mother. But she was still locked up. In a place with no voice, no spirit, no love or rage. She was a good mother, like her mother who was gone, like the mother she'd been for seven years and like all the other mothers who come and go with the seasons of life. The room then the stairs, the elevator then the bay window, the sitting room and that companion, friend, inmate, loon or whatever she was supposed to call her. Everything was white. The white made everything sterile, less motherlike. But she was impassive and kept turning everything over in her head. The room then the stairs, the elevator then the bay window, the sitting room and that companion, friend, inmate, loon or whatever she was supposed to call her. Her name was Paula and she was also a mother. And maybe someone else had also told her whether or not she was a good mother. Her name was Paula. Her name was Anaïs. They both had a name. So why were they allowing other people to tell them what names to use? Or to judge whatever it was they'd done or left undone? Of course, that was madness. And then came the day of her appointment with the psychiatrist. She walked into his white office, looking at him as if he were a stranger. Just a few signs of depression, nothing serious, announced the psychiatrist, covering his protruding belly with her file. Anaïs was still uncertain and scared; she asked questions and was taken aback, but the psychiatrist spoke clearly. The time had come for her to leave that place. She unglued herself from the white chair, looking at him as if he were a new friend. Before leaving his office, Anaïs turned back to face him. "Do you know Elisa?" she asked. He said that he did and that she'd come to ask a few questions so she could finish up her report. "However..." he trailed off. Anaïs asked him to go on: "However what?" He said that Elisa had ended up answering more questions for them than the other way around.

She waited on her feet, standing at the Centre's front door beside her rollaway luggage, when she finally saw her father's car pull up. He and Jan came into view, and she heard the sound of the brake followed by the sudden quiet of the engine as it came to a stop. She peered through the passenger door, which was ajar and dark, and then she saw Foix's little legs poking out underneath, making contact with the ground one by one. She opened her arms, relieved to see Foix's quick legs rushing toward her. She bent down to draw her into a big, unrushed hug.

The landscape flashed past the car window, and she couldn't even feel all the potholes on the national road — their presence eclipsed by her much pined-for return. Her father wouldn't stop pestering her about who'd tied her up in the shed. She kept saying she'd never tell. And her father assured her that, if that was so, then she needn't worry, as the police hadn't found any evidence at all and the case would soon be filed away. Anaïs could suddenly breathe easy, while her memory of Miquel grew all the more serene, no longer accompanied by a pang of guilt, and she thought of Elisa with a strange sense of salvation. The way one thinks of their mother. And Jan, who sat in the front seat, window rolled down, the hair on his forehead catching the wind, elbow sticking out as he gazed at the sea, smiled without uttering a word.

THE NEWSPAPER

As it so happened, the town had no time to cool off, much less forget anything. The mayors knew it, the government knew it — there was never a right time to resume construction. It wouldn't have taken long for the town to make those in power lose their patience, though. After a few attempts at restarting construction, they would've sent in the riot police and quickly put an end to the largest revolt the region had ever seen. But there was something more — something very few had predicted.

Three months of summer had drawn to an end. Elisa drank her coffee on the terrace of her go-to bar as she leafed through the paper, wetting her fingertips as she turned each page. The trial of a group of Islamists accused of terrorism had begun. And she thought that the young men likely had nothing to hold on to, no mirrors, no hope. Perhaps they had no homes. Perhaps no land to call their own, either. After Anaïs's case, she'd got used to reading between the lines. That was something she liked. She took a drag of her cigarette as she turned the page, then began reading about the forest fires devastating the country's driest regions. There was an opinion piece, abandoned farmland, drought, abandoned farmland and geographical models, abandoned farmland, with the government, and obviously the drought, at fault. The fires were madness. The attacks were madness. And she was tired of reading about tragedies. Her life was already miserable enough, she thought, a smirk on her face.

She turned her head and called the waiter over, then asked if they had any local papers. The waiter said he'd bring her one, and she thanked him. She turned her head again and shut her weary eyes, the bad news weighing down on her like a slab of stone. When she opened them again, she saw Mateu standing in the middle of the square, staring at her intently. She glared at him. There was no turning the page. Twenty smooth years of marriage. And five years of separation because he had someone on the side. She hadn't seen him in something like three years. What was the point of this strange visit? Was it worth giving him the time of day? He's back to grovel, you can bet on it, all of us women are the same to him, she thought. It distressed her. Yes, that's what it was, distress in all caps, no matter how clean-shaven, handsome, or seductive he could be. She was more important than the display he was making, showing up there like a dog. Life was more important. And she kept glaring at him. A furious and empty gaze, fishlike. And the pigeons scurried under the table. As she held his gaze, she looked down at her crossed legs, at her right heel, which hung in the air. And she shook her heel in the air to scare off the pigeons. Then she looked back at Mateu, who appeared less hopeful than before. She gave another silent, curt and brief shake of her heel, and the pigeons withdrew even farther out. Then she raised her cruel, impatient eyes again to make sure Mateu had seen how easily she'd brushed off the pigeons. Yes, he'd seen. He turned around slowly, without saying a word.

"Elisa?" said the waiter, who'd just come by with the local paper and found her staring out at the square, a delighted look on her face. "Oh yes, yes, thanks, let's see what's cooking on God's green earth," she said with a smile as she picked up the newspaper.

LOOMING ECONOMIC CRISIS TEMPORARILY HALTS CONSTRUCTION ON THE LOGISTICS CENTRE. GOVERN-MENT PAUSES ALL CONSTRUCTION PENDING ECONOMIC UPTURN. ECONOMIC RECOVERY COULD TAKE A DECADE. FORMER OWNERS PERMITTED TO FARM COMPULSORILY PURCHASED LAND UNTIL CONSTRUCTION RESUMES

THE NIGHT

He sounded the horn.

He could make out Samira's silhouette moving inside her house. She must have heard him but she was still getting ready. Bringing a cigarette to his lips, he peered at himself in the rear-view mirror, at the blond, sweaty strands of hair and the moles on his forehead. She'd like him all the same, in that usual way of hers — as a friend, a lover, someone with whom things would always be okay. Dust had settled on the glove compartment, radio and steering wheel, but the two of them were close enough that it didn't matter. As he waited, the exhaust pipe pumped out fumes, his car noisy as a city street. With one hand, he brought the lighter up to the end of his cigarette; with the other, he beckoned.

He saw her shuffle out the front door in a rush, knowing his white Corsa would provide respite from the cold now that December was imposing itself. The black leggings she'd wore to lounge around the house, her even darker, tousled hair — everything looked good on her. And messy hair suited him, too, he thought, but there was no need to make an effort anyway, since there'd be nobody else at Les Madrigueres beach. As she moved to open the door, he raised his cigarette finger to greet her, knowing that her white smile against her brown skin would make him melt. Hello, Jan. Hi, Samira. Lucky they could go out, chat, shoot the shit; lucky the unending unemployment crisis would melt him away, too, but differently.

They crossed Vilarer in second gear, without having to slow down much at stop signs and pedestrian crossings, not even at crossroads, since kids didn't really play outside anymore. They passed the last roundabout and picked up speed on the grey, potholed asphalt. Half a tire jut off the narrow road — an age-old goat path, now tarred over. Slaps on the knee, small talk, laughter and quiet. They stopped at the petrol station. Samira stepped out of the car and went into the store, quickly returning with a couple of cans.

Nothing had changed since the last time. Everything was as it was before she left. Even that September felt like the one before it. And the one before that, and the one before that. Even if they weren't like the Septembers of their childhood, the ones from beyond — the true Septembers. Since that day, the bulldozers hadn't destroyed anything else. First, the police investigation had delayed construction, then the townspeople — moved as they were by what happened — and finally, the crisis. The latest headlines were out. A temporary pause on all construction due to the looming economic crisis. A crisis that could last a decade. A decade during which farmers, like his father and Anaïs, could keep cultivating their expropriated land. Meaning the harvest was going on as usual. Its fragrance hung in the air, and the asphalt was dirty and the tractors, alive. And Jan was speaking quickly because he had to explain everything to Samira, who already knew all about it, but he had to say it in person. It was incredible, monumental, extraordinary, and she had to hear it from his mouth. He looked at her, then the road, then at her, then the road, as he slapped the steering wheel in excitement. She had to know that there was a stretch of land beneath Montmell and the Twin Mountains that would live to see another day thanks to Anaïs. Because the crisis would have postponed construction anyway, and if they'd gone through with the bulldozing, there'd have been nothing there to take its place — just a sea of hollow earth.

Les Madrigueres was emptied of visitors as September settled in. The endangered birds kept to their natural rhythms, and the dunes were taller and greener than before Samira had left for

Canada. They spread out a beach blanket and sat down next to one another. The cloudy waters guarded the rocks from a by-gone stream. The bounds of summer were palpable in the chilly evening air, and Samira was wearing a green, spaghetti-strapped dress that skimmed her brown skin. She hugged her shoulders, her beer can half buried in the sand. Their silence was comfortable. Nothing needed to be said. They already knew this was just a visit. She'd be back on her way in a few days. They knew they hadn't wasted time. There was no need to say that they'd both been with other people. That Jan hadn't found work but that he'd learned to see things with different eyes. That Samira had seen the world — how much of it Jan didn't know — but it was the same as always, just a bit different. All that had gone down with Anaïs and the Logistics Centre was behind them, and it was drawn-out and dense and faraway. Many months had gone by. There was no need for them to kiss.

"You could come with me to Canada."

"Yeah."

"We'll see when you get there." "We'll see, we'll see." They couldn't see the grey blur of Mallorca. It could only be spotted from Montmell, at dawn. The sea stretched out, infinite, before them. And everything would be alright.

There was a Saturday when they all got together to pick grapes. Samira handed him her digital camera and asked him to take a picture of her with her hat on while she held up the shears, standing between the xarel·lo vines. And she would download it to her computer and send it to her friends in Montreal. There was a small, brightly coloured hat beneath the sun, and a white, adult-sized T-shirt from a past festa major that went down to Foix's knees. There were the harvesting shears and Foix's delicate hands and Anaïs's arms wrapped around her in order to show her the best way to hold them. There was his father and Uncle

Xavier and Jaume and Víctor. And Mohamed. There was half of the shed and Anaïs's excitement about rebuilding it, and the growing pottery collection and Aunt Empar, who arrived late and moved to the side to avoid being in Samira's photo with her harvesting clothes on. A joyful harvest during which they'd all help out for a bit, under the sun, though it wouldn't be like when they were younger. Because now there were big winemakers, cheap bottles, bulk exports and the plummeting price of grapes. There was life, uprooted, liquid, the uncertain madness of each and every one of them. And smiles for the camera on that briefest of days. And papers from the Logistics Centre, undisturbed in some drawer in some office of some headquarters in some place that looked nothing like that one. Papers that neither the government nor the businessmen had torn up. Pages in black and white, never to burn like stars against the dark night, despite the small battles they'd already won.

AUTHOR'S NOTE

There's a belltower in Llorenç del Penedès with a green steeple, a road called Francesc Macià at its foot, much like in Vilarer. But Llorenç and Vilarer are not the same town. There's also a road with a faded white line running down it called L'Hostal Road (and Way), which passes through farms, vineyards and olive groves, where you can also catch a glimpse of an emblematic pine tree called the Pi de Llobets. But this isn't Quatrecases Road, even though L'Hostal is also a small neighbourhood, much like Quatrecases.

L'Hostal's landscape echoes the scenery that inspired this novel, although the town in *September and the Night* is a bit flatter and closer to the motorway exit. In both settings, the vineyard comes off as an all-absorbing sea, and the yellows, browns, greens and reds fluctuate year-round as in few other places in Catalan country.

Vilarer and Quatrecases are made-up names, but, to one side of L'Hostal, stand two identical mountains sealed together by a slope — the Gemenelles (from the Latin geminī), which are more widely known as the muntanyes Bessones, or the Twin Mountains.

Like the Twin Mountains, the rest of the places in the novel are real, though the characters who inhabit it are fictitious, and any likeness is a result of coincidence alone.

Before the 2008 crisis, there was talk of building a Logistics Centre (Centre Integral de Mercaderies) whose hundreds of acres of storage space would supplant the many xarel·lo, macabeu and parellada vineyards throughout Sant Jaume, L'Arboç and Banyeres. The project is on-going, under a new name and form, but construction has yet to start. Since then, a citizen's platform has fought against it, but it's not the same one that appears in *September and the Night.*

Thus, apart from the looming shadow of a Logistics Centre, all of the events in this novel are fiction.

ACKNOWLEDGEMENTS

Many thanks to the countless people who've read versions of this work; for the interviews and consultations; for the empathy, Tupperware meals, and all the care that it took for me to write part-time with a sense of "no-time," despite all its privileges; for being there, for understanding my being somewhat absent from our friendships and from our struggle, despite not knowing my full reasoning, during this silent and explosive task of writing.